"Brazil has a problem with femicides. It often takes years for a court case to be initiated and a few years longer if the victim was poor, Black, or indigenous. Melo makes the fates of real victims visible in her latest novel. Her determination to pursue a certain style, the freedom with which she writes confidently around generic set pieces, is evident at first glance. . . . Melo puts words into a singing rhythm, arranges them in verse so that they unfold as poems."

— *FRANKFURTER ALLGEMEINE ZEITUNG*

"Patrícia Melo's novel is a powerful plea against male violence, not a diatribe but a brilliantly composed piece of literature."

— MARCUS MÜNTEFERING, *DER FREITAG*

"Engaging and well-written, the book is the author's first to have a female protagonist. In addressing a sad reality, Melo has chosen to blend the plot with a little fable. [*The Simple Art of Killing a Woman*] is a work of fiction that depicts real-life events."

— ANA CLARA BRANT, *JORNAL ESTADO DE MINAS*

"[Femicide] is the subject of Patrícia Melo's excellent new book. . . . Based on real events in Cruzeiro do Sul, a lawyer investigates cases and hears testimonies of the tragic stories of women who have been relegated to oblivion. . . . Most striking is the metamorphosis of our rational, modern protagonist and her experience with indigenous women and their ancestral knowledge, in visions of breathtaking beauty."

— NELSON MOTTA, *O GLOBO*

"This is literature inspired by life. This is fiction constructed within the pages of a book illustrating the real events that shout every day from the pages of newspapers and news websites. Here is one woman crying out for all women. An urgent novel that galvanizes and condemns."

— *JORNAL DO BRASIL*

"With writing that is direct and at the same time strong and poetic, the author turns into literature the reality reported in newspaper headlines that are often hard to believe. From judicial and legislative issues to the first sign of violence that is silenced out of fear. The doubts, the sense of guilt, the discoveries and, after so many male voices in her works, the profusion of different female characters."

— ROBERTA PINHEIRO, *CORREIO BRAZILIENSE*

THE SIMPLE ART OF KILLING A WOMAN

PATRÍCIA MELO

THE SIMPLE ART OF KILLING A WOMAN

Translated from the Portuguese
by Sophie Lewis

RESTLESS BOOKS
NEW YORK • AMHERST

First Restless Books paperback edition November 2023

Paperback ISBN: 9781632063465
Library of Congress Control Number: 2023939505

Published by arrangement with Literarische Agentur Mertin Inh. Nicole Witt e. K., Frankfurt am Main, Germany.

Published with the support of the Swiss Arts Council Pro Helvetia.

swiss arts council

This book is supported in part by an award from the National Endowment for the Arts.

This book is made possible by the New York State Council on the Arts with the support of Governor Kathy Hochul and the New York State Legislature.

NEW YORK STATE OF OPPORTUNITY. | Council on the Arts

NATIONAL ENDOWMENT for the ARTS
arts.gov

Cover and interior map design by Sarah Schulte
Designed and typeset by Tetragon, London

Printed in the United States of America

1 3 5 7 9 10 8 6 4 2

RESTLESS BOOKS
NEW YORK · AMHERST
www.restlessbooks.org

For Celina, Maria Luiza, Renata,
Mariza, Rebecca, Luiza, and
Maria, the women in my life.

They would stamp the labia
Blossoming cheeks,
Full, high breasts, and
Proud nipples,
For afternoons of love.

— SOUSÂNDRADE

I ask no favors for my sex. . . . All I ask of our
brethren is, that they will take their feet from off
our necks.

— SARAH GRIMKÉ

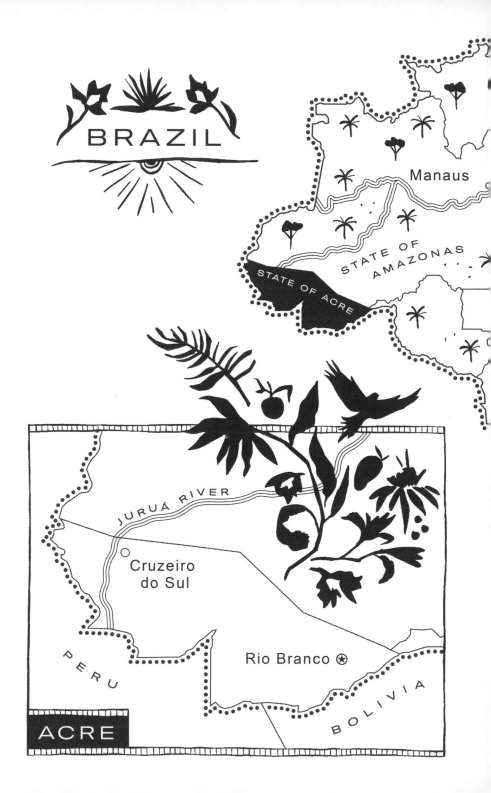

Legend has it that the world's largest tropical forest harbors a settlement composed solely of fierce female warriors: the Icamiabas. Men are only allowed to enter this settlement for the purpose of procreation, and are expelled shortly after the birth of any child— taking the child with them, should the newborn be a boy. The luckier of these men receives a green stone from the Icamiabas, a kind of talisman which ensures their good fortune and healthy lives.

Having crossed the Andes in 1542, the Spanish conquistador Francisco de Orellana describes in a letter he sent back to King Carlos I how, during his journeys by the forest's rivers, he was attacked by these brave warrior women who, according to him, fought entirely naked, armed only with bows and arrows. Upon learning of this, the king decided to name the river where the encounter had happened the Amazon, in reference to the Amazon women, the equally legendary Greek warriors, who were said to have cut off one of their breasts in order to more easily carry their quivers of arrows.

THE SIMPLE ART OF KILLING A WOMAN

1

KILLED BY HER HUSBAND

Elaine Figueiredo Lacerda,
sixty-one,
was gunned down
on her own doorstep
on a Sunday evening.

A

THE NIGHT WAS COOL AND PLEASANT. I lit a cigarette and stood with my arms crossed, gazing at the opaque sky.

"That guy is taking photos of you."

To my right I discovered a bow-tied figure leaning on our hostess's car, also smoking. Behind us, the house seemed to thump with the syncopation of the music. The man gestured at a window in the block across the road.

"There," he said.

Realizing he'd been detected, my observer vanished. The lights went out and the blind came down.

"These idiots think they can snap every pretty woman who comes out to smoke here," my bow-tied companion went on. He was quite drunk.

After a pause, he added: "You must be used to it."

From my end: silence.

"Doesn't it bother you?" he asked. "When people take photos? It must be a drag being so beautiful."

"It's a neighbors' quarrel," I said, exhaling.

"With Bia? He has a problem with Bia?"

"He was filming, didn't you see? He's going to complain about the party. The loud music."

"That kid has no idea what loud music means."

I could just see the guard beside the gate, at the road's entrance, checking cars as they arrived for the party.

"How do you know Bia?" he asked.

My cigarette burned slowly down. "We work in the same office," I said.

"Lawyers—like me?"

I dipped my head, yes.

"Don't tell me this is some kind of school reunion disco?"

I ground out the cigarette with the toe of my new shoe, trimmed with little gems, and went back into the party.

Bia was chatting with a group of friends inside the doorway. Catching sight of me, she turned and tried to drag me onto the dance floor. Even drunker than the man outside, she kept shouting in my ear, something about my boyfriend. I left her shaking her ass under the strobe lights. What happened next was one of those moments that seem to occur outside of time, as though you've accidentally crashed someone else's film.

My boyfriend appeared in the hall on his way from one of the bedrooms and pulled me into the bathroom, very worked up about something. "Who've you been with?" he yelled. "Where have you been sticking your nose?" Everything was thrumming, I could practically feel the music pulsing up through my feet, right to the tip of my tongue, and he was holding my arms down, holding me against the cold marble wall, but I said nothing, I couldn't react, I could not believe this was happening—my gorgeous partner, this deliciously sexy, cultured man with the ready laugh whom I'd only just begun to call my boyfriend a few months ago and who, till now, had been as courteous, respectful, and loving as I'd wish a boyfriend to be—this man was bellowing in a fury of wounded propriety, without the least provocation, but all I could do, while trying to get my arms free, was give a little laugh. And the tense little smile that lingered on my face seemed to fire his eyes with a wild gleam, like you see in some dogs before they attack.

Smack. Until that moment, I'd never been hit before. In the face.

"Whore," he hissed, and stormed out of the bathroom.

2

KILLED BY HER EX-HUSBAND

Fernanda Siqueira,
twenty nine,
was slashed to death with a knife
in front of her neighbors
upon returning the keys to
the apartment
where she had been living with her ex
until a few months before.

B

AND YET, A YEAR EARLIER, when it began, it was efferves-
cent, filled with laughter. You couldn't miss him. He was in
the club's garden, his forearms planted firmly in the well-kept
lawn, his muscled legs aiming into the cloudless deep-blue
sky—"a yoga inversion," he explained when he joined me in
the pool. "The blood does a kind of Roto-Rooter deep-clean
on your veins." He took another quick dive. "Clears out a lot of
bad shit."

My day job demands facing the slings and arrows of outrageous hatred and ignorance, I thought. If I try doing anything
upside down, I'll vomit up barbed wire and a whole arsenal of
nuclear weapons.

"What are you sniggering about?" he asked.

I wasn't really laughing. I had photophobia which, exacer-
bated by swimming without my sunglasses, had left a kind of
fake grimace stranded on my face.

His name was Amir and he was already part of my world: a
lawyer like me, he was a little older, divorced and, it appeared,
also a member of the Pinheiros sports club.

I had seen a few of his performances in court, prosecuting nameless criminals, and had admired his well-constructed, forceful arguments. He stood out.

Here in the water, minus the suit and the murderers he regularly demolished, and despite the teeth which could have been whiter, he seemed even more attractive. In fact, in that glorious sunshine, what I saw was a very unusual kind of guy: a yogi public prosecutor with a circus acrobat's facility for handstands.

A half-hour of conversation, and already I felt quite at ease.

After our swim, he talked about his cases—a bunch of losers, broadly speaking, these days including quite a number of Venezuelans and Haitians—and we talked about philosophy, in which he professed a particular interest. He said he'd written his doctoral thesis on Wittgenstein. I told him about my attempt to read Husserl's *Logical Investigations.*

"I gave up not far off the starting block," I confessed, "right after running into a digression on how one ought to represent a non cat upon a table. Or a cat that used to be on a table . . ."

"Vintage Husserl!" he agreed, laughing.

We were wrapped in our own bubble of hilarity. Laughing with someone is a powerful aphrodisiac.

"I've been wondering if your enthusiasm for this kind of philosophy might be what brought litigation into your life," I said. "You seem to thrive on complication."

"I'll have to watch out with you around," he replied. "Brainy women are fucking scary."

What Amir meant, of course, was that the majority of women are stupid. But under the poisonously seductive empire of my own hormones, I took no notice. Worse, I turned the signs around, transforming negatives into their opposite. Amir had an effective habit of making himself the star of every story, hammering everyone around him down to size with his tongue. I remember that an eminent sociologist was sunbathing not far from us, attracting the attention of other club regulars. He smiled at me, openly looking me up and down. "Do you like that guy?" Amir asked.

He didn't even let me reply.

"A pseudo-intellectual talking head," he said. "Look out for him. As soon as some debate about our indigenous Indians or sexual assault or racism or deforestation in the Amazon comes up, *bam*—there he is, all over the studies, research cited on TV or online, transparent as the rest of them, spotless in his red trousers, geeky specs like all the hipsters wear, taking the side that everybody takes, catching the same flak everybody catches, nailing all the same targets. Because it's 'cool' to be against what everyone else is attacking, to support who everyone's defending. It goes down well. No hard feelings. Everything he does, from an intellectual point of view, is go-with-the-flow of what should be more widely known as the cocksuckers' flock. I hate that phoney good-boy bullshit."

Later I said to my friends that Amir was a mercurial sort, a man who couldn't be typecast—and I liked it.

When I told Amir I was keen to contribute to my firm's pro bono work, he suggested that, if I was feeling guilty about earning money—which couldn't in fact be the case, for my starting salary as a lawyer was laughable—I should go into teaching.

"You wanna give something back? Get into charity?"

"It's not charity. It's an exchange of skills."

"Some exchange. So you bring your work and what do they bring—their problems? I don't believe in that. Solidarity, altruism, Father Christmas, the lottery: none of that works in this country. None of that does it for me," he said. "I prefer my dues in cash."

I giggled. I thought he was teasing, but that was just his standard line. A cheap one, too. I asked, "What else don't you believe in?"

"Better ask what I do believe in."

"Give me the list."

"Cancer, Darwin, pure math"—he paused—"and the Devil."

When we dived in again to fish out my cap, blown off by the rising wind, I could already feel an energy glowing around us.

That evening we went back to his apartment, me thoroughly toasted by the sun and he slightly tipsy from the wine at lunch. That was how it began.

You never imagine that a guy like this, a Wittgenstein reader and yoga fan, will hit you in the face at a lawyers' New Year's Eve party.

But the statistics show that it happens a lot. And that lots of men don't stop at a slap. They'd actually rather kill you.

3

KILLED BY HER EX-BOYFRIEND

Rayane Barros de Castro,
sixteen,
was shot at close range.
Before killing her, the murderer sent her
a WhatsApp:
"I'm going to live my life, but
you aren't going to live yours."

C

SLUT. COW. BITCH. The names are all variations on a theme. Bimbo. Tramp. Tart. In one case, the alcoholic husband liked to call his wife Mrs. Toad—as I read this, I recalled a photo I saw online, a close-up of a pretty woman with a proper double chin, and the caption: *Fuck it*. "Fat toad," the man called her, snorting with mirth. The victim would be moving around the house, husband stumbling after her, shouting over and over, "Mrs. Toad, Mrs. Toad, Mrs. Toad . . . ," right in front of their kids. He'd be singing, "'Croak!' said the Toad, 'I'm hungry.'" And he used to tell her, "You could squeeze two kilos of oranges in that fat jowl of yours." When he found she wouldn't rise to his mockery anymore, he attacked her, fatally, with a kitchen knife. In another case, a boyfriend took the time to warn his victim: "I'm gonna stick a bullet in your cunt." He fulfilled his promise. Yet another murderer used to tell his partner, "Luzineide, I can get bushmeat like you by the kilo, it's all there in the butcher's trash heap." She was killed by smothering. Iracema was killed by strangulation, as were Elisa, Marineide, and Nilza.

It's ridiculous to think that a murderer would even worry about the post-mortem! The system is made so it doesn't work. From the top down, whoever's investigating will look at the victim with contempt: just another woman, he'll think. A Black girl. A street girl. An object. He won't even pick up when the phone rings in the den he calls his office. Let the incident go to the next man.

They couldn't do this with my mother for some basic reasons: she was white, and she wasn't poor.

Outside the reference books, I had personally collected the details of a hundred and eighty cases, all downloaded from the judicial records of the Brazilian state of Acre which, unlike most districts in the richer states, has digitized its entire archive in a heroic attempt to shake off our national culture of state-sponsored nepotistic stalling. Wanda. Telma. Abigail. Kelly. The list of names filled my computer screen several times over, and I kept that screen open in front of me all through the flight to Acre.

Professions of the accused: soldier, electrician, builder's mate, farm laborer, civil servant, student. You could say that women-killing is a democratic sort of crime. I was making my own spreadsheets, which would later crunch these statistics into even more statistics. Education levels of the accused: semi-literate, college degree, illiterate, first-year diploma student. Degree of kinship with or relationship to the victim: husband, boyfriend, lover, ex-lover, brother, brother-in-law, stepfather. In only five of the cases, the victim had no connection at all with her murderer.

During the flight, I thought of a childhood friend who used to squash insects and stick them into a scrapbook. I even had a go at this myself, but I never liked killing butterflies. Perhaps now I could fill a few albums with my photos of murdered women—or with the murder weapons? Kitchen knives, scythes, pocket knives, spades; also bottles, hammers, electric wires, pressure cookers, and barbecue skewers. In the moment of murdering a woman, any object can be your weapon.

I only looked up from the cases when the plane stopped to land in Brasília. I watched as the other passengers disembarked, the kind of men that like to wear identical suits and carry identical laptops. How many of them also liked to assault women? The heat grew oppressive. I thought about getting up and asking the stewards to put the air-conditioning back on but I was overcome by a wave of weariness. Wanda.

Abigail. Carmen. Joelma. Rosana. Deusa. I sat there looking at all the women's names, a column of bodies that seemed never-ending. I slept.

Three hours later, I awoke in Cruzeiro do Sul, Acre's second city, without even noticing our stop in Rio Branco, its capital.

Having left Brasília quite empty, the plane was now full. While we waited to leave, I considered how many of the passengers might be the children of murdered women. Like me, they were here to watch the trials.

We stepped outside to the shock of the city's humid heat. "Proudly Acreano," the welcome sign proclaimed.

All I knew about the region was what I'd gleaned at university from reading Euclides da Cunha's books about the occupation of Amazonia in general and of Acre in particular. In them, he described a kind of "inverted natural selection" at work in this realm designated for banishment.

I grabbed a taxi and gave the driver my hotel address. *El uso del casco es obligatorio* proclaimed a sign, revealing our proximity to the Peruvian border, but no motorbiker that I could see was wearing a helmet.

"Is it your first time in Cruzeiro do Sul?" the receptionist asked. He was a good-looking, somewhat shaggy-haired mestizo named Marcos and, I would learn, the hotel owner's son.

I said yes.

"Then you have to tell your São Paulo friends that Acre really exists," he replied.

Two weeks after Amir slapped me, my firm had begun selecting junior lawyers to observe the many task forces documenting femicide trials around the country. The idea was to contribute fresh data and statistics to our senior partner Denise Albuquerque's project. Denise was writing a book on how the state creates murderers by sanctioning the asymmetry in gender relations. She summed it up by saying: "We need to talk about the state-authorized massacre of women. Ten thousand unsolved femicide cases in the courts: that is my subject."

"Where is the furthest from São Paulo that I can do this work?" I'd asked my colleague Bia, who was looking after the selection of lawyers for the mission.

"Acre," she said.

———

In the days that followed, wherever I went, Marcos would appear as if from nowhere, flanked by Tadeu, his loyal dog. I would be leaving the courthouse, or in the square eating an ice cream, and there he'd be again, emerging from the university in one of his flashy orange, violet, or hot pink T-shirts, or sometimes just barefoot and in shorts, off to swim in a stream on the city's outskirts. When we spoke, he would stare oddly, almost childishly, straight into my eyes. He walked with his feet slightly turned in, which hardly improved his machismo quota. If he was driving, he would offer me a lift. He was forever asking, "Will you come for a swim?" His mother was an indigenous woman of the Ch'aska community, he said, "So you really should come and meet the Ch'aska." Each day he would add to my list of must-dos while in Acre. "You have to walk in the forest." "You should catch a flock of kingbirds in flight." "You have to come for a swim in the Croa." "You really should try ayahuasca." If it hadn't been for his omnipresence and constant availability, we wouldn't have become friends so quickly.

On the evening of my arrival, seeing my gaze drawn to banners hanging across the hotel's balconies that proclaimed *Bienvenidos, hermanos bolivianos y peruanos*, he spent a long time explaining how living in a border town was a "really crazy thing." As he put it, "You end up not being from here or from there, but it's cool. I feel like a citizen of the world." And he pulled me into the street to look at the full moon, despite there being no moon at all.

Later, I took a shower, unpacked my suitcase, and put my clothes away. Amir had sent me another email. "So you've blocked my number? When will you stop being childish and speak to me directly?"

By eleven I was in bed, exhausted, unable to sleep. The lights on, I lay staring at the damp patches creeping across the ceiling toward the windows. And then, *smack!* I felt the slap across my face once more. The scene came to me differently now, no longer as if I were also an observer, watching myself being slapped. My fly-on-the-wall self had disappeared. I was there alone with my attacker. *Whore.* My face burned even more fiercely than it had that night.

It was exasperating to admit that I'd been thinking in circles. From the slap and back to the slap. In point of fact, a slap in the face can have the same effect as an expanding bullet. Leaving aside the obvious differences, a slap can prompt a psychological experience akin to a dumdum's impact on the flesh: instead of going clean through your body, its entire destructive energy breaks out inside you, compounding the wound. Lots of people who are regularly beaten up die at the first slap—psychologically. And yet, my slap seemed to be creating a kind of reverse effect: it seemed to be raising a piece of me that had been forgotten, something stifled inside me, a piece that on coming free, levered up another, and so on and so on, down to the last lost piece, the furthest fallen, as good as buried—the one called "mother."

My feelings about my mother's death had already been through different phases. There was the time of not wanting to forget her face, which meant making my grandmother enlarge several photos and fill our house with her likeness; there was the pre-adolescent phase of not wanting to talk about it anymore, in which all the photos were taken down except one, of her at eighteen in shorts and sneakers, sitting next to her dog. Then came the phase when I left her buried under all the layers of my own rebellion. It was only during my law-student years, at last equipped with appropriate technical vocabulary, that I could bear to return to her death, though I was still deeply wary of the facts. The words "murder," "father," "trial," and "prison" were never mentioned, and I even avoided thinking of them, as if they had some terrible power to resurrect the past.

The slap had triggered something new. It was as if the dam holding back how much I actually missed my mother had broken. Somehow, it brought us back together. What the blow had shown me was that we were made of the same stuff. For the first time, I wanted to open all the boxes my grandmother had kept clean, logged, and labelled for years, packed with enough material to fill a museum in honor of her dead daughter. All the sleepers inside me were waking, and they were hungry.

Never mess with someone who's carrying a corpse along inside them.

ALPHA

I listened to the grasshoppers whirring, the monkeys and cicadas in fearsome vocal gladiation. I thought this must be what they called the *peia*, but the jungle is noisy, Marcos explained: there's a continuous symphony of insects, the cicadas and bees, but also the birds, owls, parrots, and toucans, not to mention the tapirs, leopards, and wild pigs, it truly is an orchestra, croaking, squawking, humming, and ululating, some like to roar, others whistle, each on their own frequency, and the farther in we go, the more howling, warbling, trilling, and hissing we hear—especially at night.

You have to stay focused on the dance, Marcos said, threading his fingers through mine. One-two and left, one-two and right. Let's dance. The colors were running together in my eyes and dripping away. Yellow, red, blue, all so garish. I saw a picture of an old Black man smoking a pipe. The Virgin and Yemanjá set around a Star of David, on the altar in the entrance, in the lee of the forest. The rhythm, one-two and left, one-two and right . . . And the unending chanting: *I am drinking this drink*, one-two and left, *Which has unimaginable potency*, one-two and right, *It reveals all of us*, one-two and left, *Here at the very heart of the truth*.

I saw a hen. People hammering. One in a fit of giggles, one vomiting. One singing, another petrified. I felt a glow of heat at my right breast, a welcome presence: what was it? The older woman in ritual white-and-green dress beside me was dancing, dancing. I closed my eyes. *I rise, rise up with joy*, thoughts were coming like birds, from the heights of the forest, I couldn't keep up with them. *I rise, rise, rise with joy.* And then the warmth at my breast turned into a warm voice, *until I reach the Virgin Mary*, and then into a head of thick hair, and then into a girl with equal wealth of hair and power, armed with bow and arrows, lacking her left breast, who spoke to me very distinctly: See there, our band coming together in the lap of the jungle. We, she said, we women, Icamiabas, mothers, *cafuzas*, sisters, Amazons, Black women, Maries, lesbians, daughters, indigenous women, *mulatas*, granddaughters, white women, we feed from the Earth, shaking with hatred, conquering, let us raise the ensign of my snake-haired avenging Exu and advance on the city, bearing cocks, great rubber dicks, with heavy ordnance, let us follow you, bad man, bullshit man, exploiter, abuser, rapist, woman-beater. Murderer. Psychopath. Our business is with you, mother-killer. Devil army.

I opened my eyes. Even this wasn't the peia yet.

"Are you all right?" Marcos asked, his face very close to mine. His breath was as fresh as a child's.

"One-two and left, one-two and right," he said again. And we went on dancing.

D

YOU WANNA MAKE SHOOTING PRACTICE for a bunch of Indians? What kind of shithole is Cruzeiro do Sul? What are you doing there? But seriously—I don't think it's fair that you're treating this one shitty little misguided slap, at some crappy party, as if it were somehow a revelation of my character. What about my second chance?

Hot kisses, Amir.

PS: Nobody deserves to go to Acre!

After the slap, Amir sent me a dozen self-centered texts, all absurdly hung up on the idea that I associated his assault with him as a person. The question that kept bothering me was how he knew I was in Acre. I'd asked Bia and other friends to keep it quiet. Who had told him?

"Of course it wasn't me. What's going on?" my grandmother asked on the phone, already taking my question as if it were a metastasized nodule of my mother's death. "Did you accept this trip because of Amir? What's he done? What are you hiding from me?"

Held at bay by my cagey replies, she shot back: "Don't leave me sitting here, worrying!"

I'd learned that lesson early. Think about it this way, a soft-spoken friend of my grandmother's had said, when my grandfather died: "Now you're the single branch that's keeping your grandmother off the ground." That made sense. To bury her husband, having already buried her daughter, to picture herself alone, with no extended family and my father hanging around our house by himself, and me in that toxic phase of teenagerhood, getting bad grades at school—all that was too much for her. I could see that for myself. Suddenly all her courage had evaporated. From within that brave and chatty woman whom my grandfather used to call a force of nature, and whose black-dyed eyebrows guarded the fiercest expressions, there emerged a terribly anxious and pathologically controlling woman. Apart from keeping me fed and breathing at any cost, nothing seemed to interest her. She even left off tinting her eyebrows, which made her look oddly incongruous, as if she were bald despite a thick head of hair. She began to be fearful of stray bullets and hospitals, of the phone ringing. "It could be bad news," she would say. She began calling me all the time. I had only to leave the house for her to phone a few minutes later, afraid that "something" would happen on my way. Her "something" might be an attack, dengue fever, an accident, being run over, outright abduction, the flu, rape—as if her call could shield me from all the evil in the world—as if she were a police officer and her mission was to "cover" me amid the shootout.

She would keep our cordless telephone in her dress pocket along with her cell phone, the way cowboys have semiautomatics in their double holsters. Thus it was by means of "telephonic surveillance" that she tried to protect me from the iniquities of the world. She would call at all hours to ask in panicked tones, "Where are you?" I had to let her know when I reached every destination. From bunker 1 to bunker 2. Call her before leaving bunker 2. Secure operation, over. And call her once more during the journey, en route to bunker 3. I'm still alive, I sometimes thought about saying. I still haven't died. My life went on in brief snatches, between phone calls to my grandmother.

My father would've had to have a fatal heart attack and she submit to fear management therapy for us to return to some kind of "normal." For now, I knew that the very slightest hint of suspicion was enough to trigger a snowballing craziness in her.

That morning, I turned off my phone, hating myself for leaving her to worry. I took a shower and put on the lightest dress I'd brought with me to face the city's equatorial heat—then I got a call from the office. It was Bia.

"Are you finding crimes involving dismemberment, mutilation, and evisceration of women out there?"

"Let me just vomit quickly in the corner and I'll be with you in a sec," I answered.

"It's Denise who wants to know. She's planning a chapter on pornography as a trigger for murdering women."

"Lovely day to you too! It won't be hard to find what she's after."

"I thought porn was just a lot of ass and pussy whipped up for limp-dicked men but you'll never believe what Denise just made me read. Have you heard of this shit they call 'snuff'? Jesus! You know, like when a guy kills the woman, rips out her uterus, and then ejaculates? The guy comes holding on to her uterus!"

"Please, Bia, it's eight in the morning . . . "

"Only yesterday I thought criticizing porn risked compromising freedom of expression . . . but the guy actually came . . . "

"Bia!"

" . . . on her bloody womb!"

"Christ, Bia!" I yelled.

"Okay, okay, I've stopped. Denise's orders are for you to interview everyone: murderers, prosecutors, defense, judges, and corpses. See you."

I went down for breakfast wondering whether, when she learned of my condition as the daughter of a victim and now a near-victim myself, Denise would still let me do this work. "Of course she would," Bia had assured me the day before. "And you should ask for a raise in view of unsanitary working conditions."

4

KILLED BY HER FATHER

She had been alive for forty-eight days
when she was strangled.
At the police station, the murderer stated
he was "very angry
and thought the child
was not his daughter."

E

THE COVER STORY in the local paper was about the trials that were to begin that morning.

The photo showed three smiling boys—the eldest couldn't have been more than twenty-five—leaning on a muddy black SUV. Boots and hats. Swagger. Behind them and to the right, a little out of focus, other boys, all holding glasses of beer. The scene couldn't have been more idyllic: clear sky, blue water, the type of image that calls to mind a stack of money, rich daddy, life in hand, no worries. University students, according to the caption. Privileged boys, the obvious conclusion. Nothing here anticipated the shared psychosis that led the trio to rape, torture, and kill a teenager from the Kuratawa community.

The victim appeared in a corner of the page, her photo provided by an anthropologist who'd visited the village only days before the crime. Her name was Txupira. In shorts and T-shirt, absorbed in a game with other girls from the village that looked something like tug-of-war except they were using a long strip of vegetation for the rope. Head thrown back, black eyes sparkling in the sun, peals of laughter in the air.

As I made my way to the courthouse, I thought of the photos of my mother that had been displayed all through our house when I was little. Her wrapped in a cape on a trip to Campos de Jordão, the tip of her nose pink with cold. At her high school graduation with her friends. In the maternity ward with me in her arms. In each one, her death hung so clearly it was like another presence. The old harvester and my mother, side by side. Death and my mother had become inseparable partners in my memories. Perhaps this was why, for some time, I had nurtured a sense of myself as expert at evaluating photos like this one of Txupira, photos of those about to die upon turning the next corner, photos of the women you see in crime reports or in the trials my law firm pursued, photos showing girls brimming with life, at the beach, at parties, with friends, or unmade-up in their ID photos; lighthearted girls celebrating with their families, women with children on their laps, sitting beside their husbands, smiling from the photo frame; it was as if I could feel the warm breath of approaching death breathing out of these images, as if I had a special talent for detecting the signal no one picks up, because no one pays attention, like those car alarms no one hears any longer, they're such a regular part of our soundscape. It took me some years to realize I had no such special talent, and that my search for the signal through all these images was no more than a quasi-pathological attempt to revive old sensations connected to my mother's death.

Cruzeiro do Sul's courthouse was located in a gloomy crate of a building with a pretentious façade of concrete lozenges, every bit as ugly as the banks and shops around it, and very different from the traditional farmhouse lodge next to it, the oldest building in the city, with high ceilings and wooden railings, which nowadays houses the city museum.

I walked into the courthouse along with an elderly indigenous lady who pressed straight on down the corridors in a hurry and was surely aiming for the same trial. She was wearing a faded T-shirt with the Batavo dairy logo, a red denim skirt, and flip-flops worn very thin at the heels. A wide stripe of ochre dye ran across her wrinkled face, completely encircling her eyes. I followed her, and when we came to the courtroom I chose a seat beside her, realizing then that I was the only woman in the rows on our side of the room who did not have this bright stripe on my face. Also that these colors went some way toward restoring the dignity that this community's miserable clothing and shoes had robbed from them.

On the far side of the room sat the non-indigenous attendees. Many of them had similar body shapes to the indigenous people and some may have been *caboclos*, but the hostility filling the air between the chamber's two sides reminded me of the rivalry between Corinthians and Palmeiras supporters that I'd recently witnessed in a football stadium.

Out of politeness I asked my neighbor if perhaps my seat was reserved for someone from the village, even though I felt that this must be my place, the side where I wanted to be.

But on registering her empty expression, I grasped the full scope of her tragedy. She was there to attend the trial concerning a young person from her tribe who had died in the worst way possible, without understanding a single word.

———

Txupira's sister Janina, who had been called to testify, spoke first:

"*My fingers hurt, my feet hurt, my legs and arms hurt,* our mother would say, and it was a pain like this, particular and queasy, *Just now it was in my back, but now it's hurting me right here in my chest,* our mother would say, *it almost feels like a caninana snake pushing its way through me, only with the wickedness, too, could it be some kind of spell? Because it hurts when I raise my arms and when I lie or sit down,* our mother said. It hurt so much the old lady's tongue couldn't stand to speak any more, could only say *aie, aie, aie* . . . It was Txupira who used to prepare our mother's tea, because when Mother went all that way to visit the shaman, she would bring Txupira with her, because Txupira was older than me and she knew more and could think more. *You take the marupá leaves,* the shaman said, *fill your hands, rub and pound it with caroba, and pour water over like this, and give it to your mother to drink.* And Txupira said, *Leave it with me, pajé."*

"And the other day, when she came out of school, Txupira told Janina: *Today we must fetch the caroba husk for mother.* Janina hadn't wanted to walk in the wet forest but she also didn't want to go back to the village alone, because it was raining and Janina was afraid of thunder, even after Txupira had explained that thunderclaps were just the great rumbling of God's sneezes, so that day which looked like night, *rumble,* and they still had no caroba, Txupira went farther, because the caroba is farther in, nearer the river, because the foliage is not the same there, the jungle only grows thinner, only sparser, *Just a little farther,*

Txupira said, *just a tiny bit more, only that far*, their feet were sinking into the mud, the trees closing around them, and Janina, silent, with the mud up to her ankles, was terrified, and wanted to go back, *Wait here then*, Txupira said, *rumble, I'll go by myself*, and she went on and on and disappeared. At first, Janina could hear her sister's steps crunching along, shuffle, crunch, shuffle, and then just the rainwater falling, falling. And then she heard a scream and a car engine starting up. And she was frightened. Janina waited and waited, the rain stopped and started and stopped again but Txupira never came back."

Some of the people of the Kuratawa community spoke Portuguese or Spanish, but not Janina. Like most of the people from her village, she spoke one of the Panoan languages, and was interpreted by an activist from the indigenous youth center.

The translator's long pauses and hesitations made me think she might not be very proficient in the language. It took me a while to see that her biggest difficulty was holding back her tears. She didn't always manage.

Janina, on the other hand, remained serene.

When it was the prosecution's turn, the noise of the car starting that Janina claimed to have heard became the focus of the questions.

"Janina did not dream up that noise," the young prosecutor, Carla Penteado, insisted, in her São Paulo accent. Her mass of curly hair and her pretty, unadorned face made her an attractively straightforward figure.

"This was not some 'jungle sound,' as the defense is absurdly attempting to frame it. This vehicle, which was covered in

Txupira's blood, has already been documented in the legal proceedings."

So it was that I learned the details of the gas station attendant's statement.

It was this man, José Agripino Ferreira, who had taken the case to the police, shortly after being asked by Crisântemo Alves to wash his Mitsubishi 4x4. Crisântemo had been arrested on the spot and confessed to Txupira's murder, also implicating two of his friends, the same pair I'd seen in the photo in that morning's paper.

According to Crisântemo, he and his schoolmates, Abelardo Ribeiro Maciel and Antônio Francisco Medeiros, had been on their way to Crisântemo's father's farm when they saw Txupira walking through the forest, beside the road. Their plan had been to go and play pool at the farm, where they would be free to dip into his father's whisky, but then the Indian girl had shown up. He'd put on the brakes.

"Jungle booty ahoy," one of them said.

"That's what I call one foxy native," said another.

"*Now* it's party-time!" said the third.

They thought it was funny: the Indian girl right there, ripe for the picking. When they called, Hey, here girl, come here, they said, the wild girl took to her heels. So one of them had to go after her, to hunt the girl down and shove her into the car. Not to rape or kill her, but to have some fun, because they found it funny seeing the Indian take fright, like an animal; they found it funny though they couldn't say why, perhaps because they were already drunk, and later, she couldn't follow diddly squat of what they said, just sat there looking at them all wide-eyed, like she had gone silly, had lost her mind, and this too they found very funny, and then—he couldn't explain how it all happened but it just did, one thing led to another, she wouldn't stop screaming and because of that they tore off her shirt and gagged her with it. All this inside the car. Then she had her breasts out, and Txupira was a very pretty Indian, and then they arrived at the farm, and all that, they went on drinking, and the thing happened, well, let's say, it all happened "naturally," you know? Antônio put his hand on Txupira's breasts, and would you believe the crazy woman gave Antônio a slap in the face? Because of that she got her hands tied up but the idea was not to rape her, 'course not. Or torture! But that little Indian, fuck me, the girl was fucking furious, even with her hands tied, seriously, she started kicking them. Then Abelardo came out of the kitchen with a knife, not to kill her, not even torture, it was just to give her a shock, and Crisântemo said he was worried their game might leave marks on the living room carpet—his mother would go off her rocker—so they all ended up in the barn, where they hung Txupira from one of the butcher's hooks to "calm her down." But the idea hadn't been to kill her, nor to rape her. It just happened. Crisântemo even thought about offering her some money, poor thing. The problem was she died before he could. Then they had to throw her body in the boot of the car—the same car that José Agripino later washed.

Txupira's family and others from her village had already turned the forest upside down looking for the girl. Her father had gone to Funai, the National Indian Foundation, to ask for help. And even before the police found out about the car and the blood, and picked up the boys, Txupira's body was discovered—she was floating on her back in the creek with her arms tied. Her nipples had been removed. And in her uterus they found splinters of glass.

5

KILLED BY HER EX-LOVER

T.R.T.,
straight chestnut hair,
irises also chestnut,
the necropsy analysis found
her body in generalized rigor mortis
and eleven wounds
with regular edges in:
the right thorax (2 cm)
right arm (2 cm, 0.5 cm)
left carotid (2 cm)
left arm (2 cm)
right thigh interior (1.5 cm)
right thigh exterior (1.5 cm)
left iliac fossa (1 cm)
frontal lobe (2 cm)
right parietal lobe (6 cm)
left parietal lobe (2 cm).
Son of a bitch!

F

THAT NIGHT, IN THE HOTEL RESTAURANT, I was startled by an icy tap on my shoulder. Juan, the hotel owner and Marcos's father, apparently thought that touching a chilled glass to my back was a friendly way to start a conversation.

His gelled hair and geometrically trimmed goatee stood out so much, they gave him a surreal, cartoonish air. He offered me *cupuaçu* juice, which he brought over himself. Then without further niceties, he sat down at my table and began to discourse upon the local fruits: the *sapota* was sweet, the rambutan sweet and fleshy, the *pitomba* was succulent and sweet, the *camu-camu* more sour than sweet, and the *maná-cubiu* very *ácida* and so many other flavors, *la niña tiene que conhecer*—you really ought to try them. And all the *belezas* of the state? A lecture about Acre as the navel of the world. I noted that he did not speak fluent Portuguese. Actually, he didn't really speak Spanish either. From what I could glean, he was forgetting his Spanish and not replacing it with any Portuguese.

"What have you come here for, *niña*?"

When I told him I was following the trials being held at the district courthouse, his smile and courtesies vanished.

"Our crimes, it seems, are different from the crimes in your part of the world, *en tu terra*?"

Not when it came to killing women. Or rather: not if we took into account the suffering women were going through before their murders. Nor the instruments used by the murderers. By these criteria, the assassination of women in Acre is no different from the assassination of women in the rest of Brazil. There are just more of them. But I wouldn't be drawn into details, and made do with pulling a grim face.

"What will you be doing with *essus informaciones*?" he went on.

"The firm I work for is organizing a book on the subject."

"Hmm. You have come here to talk about our problems?"

Silence. I spotted the hotel cook's teenage son, Zenóbio—whose roles included bellboy, receptionist, and waiter, by turns—and asked him to bring my bill.

As silence gathered thickly around our table, I felt as though I was being weighed before my slaughter.

"I wonder why you are not writing about the crimes of *tu ciudad*. Don't you live in *San Paolo*? That's the true jungle of Brazil."

My bill signed, I thanked him for the juice and headed to my room, feeling his butcher's eyes fixed on my bottom. But the worst part of the night was still to come—by email.

My darling kryptonite, here I am, I can't work, I can't sleep, I can't do fuck all.

The difference between me and all these women who ended up stabbed, mutilated, cheated, and poisoned in the trials and in the books I went around reading, my advantage over all these women like Txupira who were raped, killed, and dumped in creeks was that I knew what to call this: level two. I had read quite a lot about how these woman-killers' emotions generally worked. The sport of killing women develops like a video game: in levels. After beating their woman, after getting drunk and trashing the place, the killers waste a good few hours trying to convince their partners they're still the loving, lovable guys of that first encounter. This lays the groundwork for moving to the next level, in which beating her turns into torture, with the use of kitchen knives, fish-gutting knives, electric wires, boots, saws, lighters, or any other objects that can pierce, cut, fracture, or burn her. Some guys can be very original, like the guy who drowned his wife in their bathtub. But that's the final stage, the cherry on the cake of violence. In earlier levels, the perpetrator always tells the victim that her days are numbered: "You're going to die," he'll say, no metaphorical fancy-work required. He drinks and tells her: "You're about to die." But before that, he'll beat her. Sometimes, even without a drink. He'll burn her with his cigarettes. He'll rape her. Slice a few strips off her body. Toss the girl down the stairs, break her arms, her legs, all the time warning: "You're going to die!" In the world of work, this has a name: prior warning.

We are looking at Amir's next level, I thought. I was hoping the rest of his message would maintain the tone of "my darling kryptonite" and wind up with pleas for forgiveness and promises of future happiness. But the following is what I read: *Your grandmother, whom I admire very much and whom I've always loved as if she were part of my own family—you know how much I mean that—told me about your mother . . .*

In disbelief, I reread the end of the sentence: . . . *told me about your mother.*

I went to the bathroom thinking I was going to faint and lay down on the tiles. It felt as though something had been torn from me; something precious had been stolen.

Abruptly, the scene came back to me. The wooden floor, my bare, dirty feet—I must have been three or four years old, I was running after the dog, his name was Tintin, when I heard my mother's voice. Suddenly, there she was, walking into that new house my father had. Beautiful, her black dress with the white spots, sunglasses perched on her head. Long black hair, just like mine. "Come and give me a cuddle," she said, and wrapped me in her arms. I smelled the same sweet, warm fragrance that lay deep in the white dressing gown with yellow flowers, which I'd kept hanging behind my bedroom door for many years after her death. "Gather your things," she said, "we're going home." I ran to my new room, in that strange house my father was living in, hunted for my sandals, my fluffy wolf, my rucksack; then, ready to go, I bumped into my father in the corridor, coming out of his room. He squatted down to speak to me. "Let's give your mother a nice surprise," he said. "Go into your room and only come out when I tell you, okay?" I froze, not wanting to obey him. "To your room," my father said. It was all very simple, very clear, very easy: I just wanted to go with my mother. "Do as I tell you," he said, impatient now.

I got up slowly, as if I'd been punched and laid out on that wooden floor, as if I had first to go via some reassembly stage to reunite my pieces, put each piece back in its place, before I could return to the room and call my grandmother.

"How could you do this to me?" I asked when she picked up. She gave a long sigh.

"My good God!" she said. "It didn't cross my mind that Amir might not know."

Then she told me how she'd been worried the last time we'd spoken. "You know I do get anxious," she said, "you know all about that. I am very anxious and full of worries." She said her head had been topsy-turvy since I'd implied that Amir had upset me; that the mere possibility of Amir being abusive had completely destroyed her sleep and her appetite, and then, Amir happened to call her, and indeed there was scope in her relationship with Amir for him to call her like that, yes, they were friends after all, wasn't he always in and out of the house, when we were dating? And Amir had been very kind, he'd asked after me, she had even suggested they get a coffee, and the two of them had ended up meeting at Le Vin, close to her home, and their conversation had been very friendly, Amir had said he loved me very much, he really did love me, said I was afraid of letting our relationship grow more serious and that was why we'd split up, and it was in that context that she'd mentioned our past and was stunned to discover he knew nothing at all about it, absolutely nothing, and she saw how shocked he was, and then she felt even more desperate than Amir, so she left convinced that I needed help and she realized I'd found it hard to talk about this with her, well, that she really did understand, I was trying to spare her the pain. "Your grandfather also didn't like to talk about it. Families that go through our kind of tragedy often wrap themselves in silence," she said, "I understand that." She said she could understand this and many other things, she understood I had a terrible void inside me, and that I was afraid of trusting people, men especially, this she could well understand, understood it perfectly, really, understood it completely, but she still didn't get why on Earth I hadn't told my partner, my long-term partner, with whom I had even considered sharing a home, that my mother had been murdered.

I didn't know what to say. Maybe having a mother who'd been murdered was my secret identity. It was the black hole of my life. Throughout my adolescence, I knew exactly how far my relationships would go: to the point when they asked, "How did she die?" That question was the barbed wire that separated me from the rest. Nobody made it beyond that point. I'd never wanted to be that person for whom the line "her mother was murdered" becomes a kind of compulsory gauntlet. Murdered by her own father. *Her father killed her mother, see?* In a single sentence my origins would implode. My family. My story. They'd put a label on my forehead: murdered mother, murderer father. Of course I had told a few people about my mother. A few. Of course I might have told Amir one day, had he not fucked everything by hitting me at that party and calling me a whore.

"Are you ashamed?" my grandma Yolanda asked. "Is that it?"

And then she began to say that she was the guilty one: for not sending me to a therapist. She had respected my preference to avoid therapy when I was a teenager, but that had been a mistake. A silly mistake.

"My God, it all happened so long ago," she said. "I should have made you do therapy, psychoanalysis, all of that. I say this out of my own experience. Without my therapy, I would still be living with that hollow feeling in my chest, the panic, the emptiness, the broken connections, that sense of being adrift like an astronaut. Did I tell you about the interview I watched with a guy who explained what had happened to Armstrong and the other astronauts when they returned to Earth? They had lost that sense of safety we feel when we leave home, the certainty that we'll go out and come back soon, the certainty that this is our solid Earth, without which we wouldn't be getting up in the morning. Your mother's death did that to me," she said. "The carpet was pulled from under me. Every time you were out of sight, I would panic. It was as if nothing in my world could be relied on anymore. Everything became life-and-death. I know we're all going to die one day, that everything comes to an end, the water on our planet will run out, the money runs out, friendships end, marriages end, but I lost it, I'd be looking at your grandfather and thinking he was going to die, everyone was going to die, I was eaten up by that 'going to die.' Without the therapy I'd be in the loony bin. Or the graveyard! How is it we never discussed this?" she asked. "Therapy saved me. Analysis is like aspirin. Like the smallpox vaccine. Do you stop taking vaccines? If I'm better today, if I'm able to see your mother's death as something in the past, it's because I did therapy."

That evening, I finally saw the difference between us. For my grandmother, my mother's death was a fact in the past. For me it was different: what I am, as in that poem, what I am is having lost my mother. What I am is having a father who killed my mother. My mother's death was more than my identity: it was a bomb welded to my body. All you had to do was raise the subject. I did not want to discuss it, not with anybody. Somehow, I managed to explain this to my grandmother. Not in any logical or linear way. I cried like a kid, like I hadn't cried in a long time. And when I stopped crying and was standing there helplessly hiccupping, she asked me:

"What are you doing out there in Acre, anyway?"

And gave me no time to reply.

"It's no good becoming a lawyer, it's no good being out there, following these cases of women who died like your mother," she said, "if you haven't learned the first lesson from this story: our silence is bullshit. Your mother died because of the silence. These women died because they weren't able to speak. Not speaking," she said, "is the tragedy."

I don't know how we finished the conversation. But I do know I did not tell her that Amir, whom she liked so much, Amir with whom I'd been in love, that Amir had slapped me in the face.

G

"I'D LIKE TO WARN YOU that the photographs you're about to see show very disturbing scenes," Carla Penteado, the young prosecutor, announced. It was the last day of hearings for Txupira's murder. Carla asked the forensics lab to present the material to the jury. Then she suggested that the translator explain what was about to happen to Txupira's mother, who was sitting in the front row, so she could be shown out of the room if she wished.

When the old lady left, all the women of her village followed, leaving the section reserved for the public half-empty.

The gentle, bright-eyed indigenous girl who had decorated the pages of the local press thanks to an anthropologist's quick camera-work, with scarlet macaw and curassow crest feathers decorating her slight frame, appeared to have nothing in common with the lump of bloody meat the lab photos offered us. Her face was disfigured, her mouth gagged. Two ribs had been broken. There were welts all over her back, belly, neck, and chest. Her hands were tied and front teeth smashed in.

Some in the jury had to look away.

Carla told the court that one of the defendants—Crisântemo—had withdrawn the confession he'd signed at the police station. There had been many details in it that coincided with the forensics' findings, and which could not have been invented by someone with no involvement in the crime.

Before the session, the smartly suited and coiffed defense lawyer, Robson, had asked the judge on the case to call Carla in for a private conversation.

"Is this a costume?" Robson had asked. "You're not telling me this is some new kind of makeup."

Carla had walked into the courtroom with the upper half of her face painted in the striking style of Txupira's villagers. She explained that the villagers' rituals maintained a profound connection with their deceased relatives, and that the paint, applied minutes earlier by the community's women in the ladies' bathroom using dye extracted from *urucum* or natural annatto they had brought for this purpose, in fact represented an important funeral ritual in the lives of the Kuratawa.

"To my knowledge, our colleague does not belong to any of their tribes."

"They're called communities," Carla corrected him. "It's a gesture of solidarity."

"We are not taking part in primitive rituals," Robson said. "Our colleague is using this stratagem to incite the sympathy of the jurors and the press, thereby breaking a fundamental rule of the Tribunal, according to which all parties must be treated equally."

The judge agreed, and ordered Carla to remove the dye from her face before proceeding with the hearing.

Carla herself told me this story later. There was an immediate understanding between us. I asked where she was from, to confirm what her accent had already revealed. "I'm from Mooca, in São Paulo," she said. "When I was transferred here, I didn't know jack shit about Acre, so I started reading everything I could get my hands on. It was as though I had parachuted back to school and was studying the history of Brazil all over again: Indian lands, virgin forest, white man arriving and fucking it up, that old routine we know so well. Except that here, this was only yesterday, in the twentieth century. The men came this way from the North-East, escaping the drought, looking for work on the rubber plantations, and they came alone—no women. They knocked off indigenous women left, right, and center. Women were luxury items, and they were ripe for stealing: from their fathers, from their husbands, from the villages. And they were sold. You could buy a woman for the price of 500 kilograms of rubber. So I thought, fuck—me the hothead with a sharp tongue, living off my own money, never backing off for anyone, still single, no kids, and my heart full of hate to lean on, I could go and work in this place where only yesterday women were being hunted down and beaten, here in the forest. Where women were sold, bulk-ordered, and stolen—how about it? This will not go easy for Acre, I thought to myself." She gave a great sonorous, almost scandalous guffaw. "I do like being a stone in people's shoes round here."

I'd introduced myself to her in the courtroom, shortly after the judge's announcement that the court would adjourn for deliberation and the sentence would be issued the following morning.

"Are you hungry?" she asked. "Want to join me for a pizza?"

I thought we'd go to a restaurant in town, but Carla took me to her house, a cool, welcoming place with a view of the Juruá river, where she showed me a saucepan full of highly aromatic tomato sauce and a dough she had prepared the night before.

"My grandparents are Italian; my pizza has to be the real thing," she explained, bringing me a bottle of wine to open. "I'm a lazy cook, but after a day like this one, I need to chop, crush, and beat something hard to calm down," she said, kneading the dough with rapid movements.

The last day of hearings had been a long one, with several tense moments for the prosecution.

José Agripino, the puny, buck-toothed gas station attendant who had reported Txupira's murderers, had been summoned to testify at the start of the session. He was like a frightened rabbit; at times, it was clear he didn't fully understand the questions. Otherwise, he told his story simply and directly for the prosecution. He said that on the day after Txupira's disappearance, some indigenous people from the Kuratawa village had come to the gas station on highway 317 where he worked, and had shown him a photo of the teenager.

"I spent a while looking at the girl," he said. "Feeling sorry for her, you know? I was looking at the little Indian girl there, smiling, poor thing, playing, poor thing, and I thought about all the blood in Crisântemo's car. I felt, well, something really bad, you know?"

But if Agripino did well for the prosecution, he did even better for the defense.

"At what time on the fourth did my client arrive at the gas station with the pickup for you to wash?" Robson had asked.

"End of the evening. I mean, around seven o'clock, right?" Agripino replied.

"So it was dark. Even so, you were able to notice that there was blood in the car?"

"On the bodywork, yes, Senhor, it was slimy the way blood gets, all splashed around, you know? Like dried jelly, you know? But it was blood. Before I washed it down, course."

Referring to photos of the gas station at the same time of night and pointing out the very limited lighting, Robson discounted the possibility of Agripino's having any decent visibility while washing the car. He went on:

"Even while suspecting there was blood on the car, instead of calling the police, you washed the pickup."

"He ordered me to wash it. Crisântemo, right? He ordered me to."

"My client is not your boss, by any chance?"

"No, Senhor."

"Therefore you were not obliged to obey him. You could have called in the police before washing the vehicle."

"Yes Senhor, good idea."

"But you did not in fact follow this course of action?"

"Only the next day."

"After you had washed the car."

"Only when the Indians came looking for me and I figured things out better. I was scared, you know?"

"What were you scared of?"

"Someone might say I knew but I didn't tell, you know? Later they might say I didn't tell. They would say that if I didn't tell."

A few people in the room sniggered.

"Could you be any clearer?" Robson asked.

"They would say I knew."

"Who is 'they'?"

"Crisântemo and his friends."

"That you knew what?"

"What should I know?"

More giggles. The whole court could see Agripino was screwing up.

Robson continued: "You said you were afraid Crisântemo would reveal what you knew. What did you know?"

"About the blood, of course. And what if there was a crime? That's what I thought. What if they killed the girl?"

"Would you mind kindly reading this document," the lawyer requested, handing a paper to the gas station attendant.

"I can't read, no."

"It happens to be a veterinary prescription," Robson said, passing the document to the jurors. "My client drove his dog to the vet that afternoon. The blood our gentleman saw was that of my client's dog. Blood that, had he not washed it off, could have been analyzed by forensics, in order to prove it was not that of Txupira."

"I can't answer to that myself, because it's you Senhor who says so."

"Senhor Agripino, is it true that you have worked for my client's father?"

A pause. The answer was a surprise.

"Yes, Senhor. Back when, must be a couple of years back, you know?"

Agripino had been employed at Crisântemo's father's timber plant. From that point on, Robson was home and dry. He demolished the witness's credibility entirely.

Agripino had sworn that his connection with Crisântemo's father "was in the past" but, as ever, the defense had the advantage of not having to prove the defendant's innocence. It had only to sow doubt.

"You can bet, when I make a few phone calls tomorrow, I'll find out all that was pure pantomime," Carla said now. "And in a few days' time, good old Agripino will be showing up in town with a lot of spending money." She laughed when she saw I had only managed to pull half the cork out, leaving the other half stuck inside the bottle. We pushed it down into the wine and I filled our glasses. Little crumbs of cork floated in the liquid.

"I was just waiting for them to call Txupira a tramp and an opportunist slut," I said.

It was true that, instead of attacking Txupira's credibility, the defense had tried to convince the jury of the defendants' exemplary record. Teachers had been summoned to corroborate this. The accused were presented as amiable and good-natured boys, "liked by all." "He's a gentleman," said the professor of farm animals' anatomy. "I can only say of him that he's a sweetheart," gushed Joslaine, a girlfriend of one of them, who arrived as if to a gala event in high heels and a gold-trimmed jacket. "Crisântemo knows how to treat a woman. He couldn't hurt a fly, never mind kill an Indian!"

Another defendant's future mother-in-law, owner of a breeding stables, explained how happy it made her horses when the boy came by. "You ought to see it!"

After a while, Robson turned back to the jury.

"Please ask yourselves why on earth these young men, of good families, all of them good-looking, with beautiful girlfriends and glittering futures ahead of them—why would they kidnap, torture, and kill an Indian woman?"

"For fun," Carla had said, when she could get a word in.

What really happened, Carla told me, was this:

"After they indulged themselves with Txupira, after they killed the girl in the worst way imaginable and dropped her body at the source of a creek, Crisântemo and his two pals took the pickup to be washed down at the gas station where Agripino was working. They knew Agripino and they gave him a good tip, thinking he would know to keep his mouth shut. Except, more than anything, Agripino was a wimp. He'd never liked Crisântemo, who probably lorded over him when he was working for the rich kid's dad, something Crisântemo, being raised to throw money at every problem, likely didn't

51

remember. But Agripino was sore. Did he rat to get revenge? Probably. And when he realized he might even get some cash out of it, he decided to help the defense. In the Labor Courts there were records of a case in which Agripino went up against Crisântemo's dad and it ended with a payoff out of court. A guy like Agripino makes no inroads among those types. It was clear the defense preferred an angle that was, let's say, more media-friendly. More environmentally attuned. It was pure strategy that stopped them attacking Txupira's reputation. For them, the indigenous people are animals. The Indians are animals. And animals are the environment. We're not about to turn this case into an eco-crime, they decided. It'll end up costing us much more. This thing of killing 'Indians' and monkeys on the verge of extinction could end up in the international press; it could turn into a hell of a row. Besides, they had Agripino, cheap little bugger, in their pockets, happy to go clowning for the jury."

I liked Carla's style. She was outspoken, almost aggressive, and yet, despite shocking levels of violence in her working day, she maintained a sunny, positive outlook. She was confident the boys would go down the next day.

"The jury-led trial is the only legal space where justice can truly be served in this country," she said. "I still believe that."

Her interventions had been very effective that day.

"I want to remind you why we are here today. We are here because a girl who was only fourteen years old"—at this, she took the newspaper photo of Txupira playing tug-of-war out of her file and held it up—"this girl was raped, tortured, and killed by three boys. It is their crime that we are judging today. It is of no interest to us if any of them got ten out of ten in an anatomy test for domestic livestock. Nor even if any of them send roses to their girlfriends. What we are judging here is not how they have treated their horses but the crime that they have committed."

Next, Carla went on to show the jury the spikes of glass found in Txupira's vagina. One of them included the corner of a Chivas Regal label. Three bottles of that whisky had been found by police investigators searching the farmhouse.

It was almost midnight when Carla's boyfriend Paulo joined us at her house. Unlike either of us, he was a local man. He talked about Santo Daime, the sacred drink imbibed in the heart of the jungle, and about the region's indigenous communities the same way a native of Rio de Janeiro talks about Sugarloaf Mountain and Christ the Redeemer.

I told them that, only a few days earlier, Marcos and I had visited a religious gathering in the forest and partaken of the Santo Daime, explaining that Marcos's mother was an indigenous woman who lived in an indigenous community, and that he had promised to take me to an ayahuasca tea ritual. Although I was more interested in the drink's shamanic background than the experience.

"Same for me," Carla said. "I'm not into this mishmash of Ave Marias and hocus pocus."

Paulo shifted uneasily. "You don't know what you're talking about," he said. "People think you just go there and take the

Daime and then you get the experience. No one invites anyone to go to Daime. Daime calls people—it's a summons. The power of Daime doesn't come to people who don't measure up. Only to those who deserve it."

"What are you on about?" Carla needled him. And to me: "When the effects of the tea wear off, he smokes a pipe out there, and gets back here high as a kite."

"I've not been to Daime this evening," he retorted.

Paulo seemed a little delicate, somehow. The asymmetry between the couple was noticeable. Carla was the elder one, independent and brilliant. But there was no doubting the sexual energy between the two of them.

"Have you experienced *miração*?" he wanted to know.

I was already a little tipsy, so I described my visions of the allegorical feminist parade, complete with giant rubber dicks. Carla laughed like a drain.

The night air was cool and pleasant. I walked back to the hotel with my head full of wine.

Don't get me mixed up with your dad . . . Some lines, fragments of phrases, on the screen of my phone . . . *lack of trust* . . . were moving too fast for me . . . *self-confidence totally fucked* . . . flashed like arrows at my eyes . . . *all this shit of ours* . . . before I could delete them . . . *I could get on a plane now* . . . Now Amir, now Grandma. *Can we talk?* All straight in the trash.

One advantage of working with real-life criminals is that the immersion in misfortune makes you reflect continually on your own good fortune. Even when the victims' stories are similar to or worse than your own, what you see in court forces you to admit that your personal dramas are not quite such an emergency, given that you still have a pulse. From this angle, our kind of advocacy was like a sudden piercing toothache which left my chronic existential back pain far in the background.

My aching calves reminded me why Cruzeiro do Sul was known as the city of steps. The Goat Steps, the Ramela Steps, the Kibe Steps, the Glória Steps. As I tramped up the São José Steps, I turned to look behind me and saw the Juruá river. Its mud-thick waters were less lovely by daylight.

From almost everywhere I walked, you could see the German cathedral, built a century ago. I used it to find my bearings. Without beauty or charm, it was just a vast barnacle on an octagonal base.

The streets were deserted, and it occurred to me that in São Paulo I would never undertake such a route on foot, after midnight. "Don't be deceived by our bucolic appearance," Marcos had said. "This is frontier country; a lot of drugs come through here. And guns."

But I felt safe in the city. Perhaps because I didn't know it well enough. Or because the first thing you learn when you dive into the world of femicide is that dark streets, deserted alleys, and dodgy neighborhoods are not genuinely dangerous places for us. The truth is that there's nowhere more perilous than our own homes. The majority of the cases I was to encounter in the weeks that followed worked like that, too. Marriage is Russian roulette for women.

Before I got into bed, I realized there was no water in my room. I called reception but no one answered.

I went to sleep with a dry mouth and a head thick with wine, spinning, spinning, spinning.

6

KILLED BY HER HUSBAND

Her skin was lovely like
a white rose petal,
but we know from the papers that, when they
fought,
he used to call her
albino gobshite.
The police suspects that
Tatiana Spitzner, 29, a lawyer,
did not commit suicide
but was thrown from a fourth-floor window
by her husband, Luís Felipe Manvailer.
Images from the security cameras show
Tatiana
being beaten in their car,
being chased through the garage
and assaulted inside the lift.
Neighbors heard her shouting for help.
They also heard the dull thud
of her body hitting the tarmac.

H

. . . FALLING, FALLING, FALLING . . .

. . . but now I was clinging to the trunk and roots of an old tree, looking down into a deep canyon, then at Amir's boots crunching through the shale. Actually, I wasn't slipping, but Amir was treading on my hands, pushing my arms away, launching me into the void, and during my fall, I still had time to think, "What a handsome bastard," falling, falling, falling until I awoke in a fright, wet through with sweat, my throat burning and with the parched mouth of a hangover. It was ten till four in the morning and I felt fuzzy from the excess of wine the night before. I called reception again to ask for water, but once more nobody answered.

I pulled on my jeans and a shirt and went in flip-flops down to the front desk.

This was the first night since coming to stay at the hotel that I'd found the desk area deserted.

I went up to the restaurant on the first floor, following the sweet scent of ripe fruit, perhaps mangoes or jackfruit, mingled with the smell of the wax they used on the floorboards. The best features of this little hotel tended to come via my nose. I tried to remember if there was a fridge from which I could grab a cold drink.

The wind was whistling outside with much braggadocio, heralding more rain and drowning out the sound of my steps. The lights were off in all the common spaces but I saw that one remained on, at the back, in the kitchen.

I walked slowly toward it and then, nearing the door, was shocked to see, sitting around the great table beside the sink, three jurors from Txupira's case along with Robson, the defense lawyer. They were drinking beer.

"The problem with this country is race," one said. "In my view, the only way is to knock it all down and start again from scratch."

Without thinking, I got my phone from my pocket and took a few photos of the little party before retreating.

It's the legal duty of all jurors to remain out of communication during the course of a trial. Court officials are likewise responsible for guaranteeing that no interaction between the members of the jury takes place. If these jurors were staying at the hotel because of the length of the trial, what the hell was this little subcommittee up to?

I was making my way back up to my room, fearful of being spotted, when I came across Juan.

"Anything wrong, *chica*?" he asked.

In the darkness, his goatee, which had seemed ridiculous at first, now lent him a demonic aura.

Perhaps I took too long to answer and this gave him time to grow inquisitive.

"I was just going to reception . . . to ask for water," I muttered.

What I said didn't make much sense, as my room was in the opposite wing, and there was no reason for me to take this staircase if I was aiming for reception.

"You can return to your room. I will bring a bottle up to you."

Just as I was locking myself in, a huge cloudburst let loose over the city. I had been in Acre long enough to know that the gales that time of year had nothing in common with the tropical storms we were used to elsewhere in the country. Here it was like a trailer for the end of the world, almost always preceded by a kind of suspense, as if, suddenly, every single heartbeat had been forced to pause. In an instant, the sky would fill with a dense, low ceiling of black cloud, the temperature would spike, the pressure plummet, and the noise and fury of the wind and thunderclaps would ring through your body. You'd feel so tense that, when the torrent finally descended and flooded the city, all you wanted to do was yell with relief. And then everything would stop working.

I tried to call Carla but my cell phone couldn't pick up a signal. The hotel's phone lines were dead. When the lights went out, Juan knocked at my door.

"I've brought water for you, *chica*."

"Leave it there, please," I answered.

I realized I was afraid of Juan, and of the men in the restaurant. They were in league with each other, I had no doubt. Juan had allowed this encounter to happen in his kitchen. He was complicit, and I had caught them in the midst of it.

I sat on the bed, trying to calm down.

Juan spoke again. "I've brought you a lamp."

I went to the door, where I could hear his heavy breathing on the other side.

"You don't want a lamp?"

"I'm on the phone," I lied.

A few seconds later, I heard his steps drawing away from the door, in no hurry.

I went to the window, feeling my heart's accelerated pulse at my temples.

When the rain stopped, daylight was already showing. But I only left my room once I'd heard movement among the other guests.

I am a caboclo of the jungle, my feathers are macaws', my bow is peach-palm, my arrows are of taquara bamboo—the music blasting from the taxi's radio was too loud even to think through.

As it wasn't yet eight in the morning, I thought I'd catch Carla at home before she left for work. On the way, I kept trying her number, but the call invariably went to her voicemail.

With the face of someone only just sprung from his bed, Paulo opened the door, in shorts and flip-flops.

"She's gone already," he said, trying to smooth his hair back. "I just made a pot of coffee, would you like a cup?"

I excused myself and hurried away, hoping to catch the taxi that had dropped me there moments earlier, but was now turning the corner.

I had to walk the whole way to the town center, which meant I saw the extent of the storm's destruction. Streets and pavements throughout the district were submerged in water. Traffic lights had stopped working and fallen trees were blocking smaller roads and avenues alike.

At the courthouse, because of the rain, there were fewer people in the public seats than the day before, but the residents of Txupira's village were all there, quite as drenched as I was.

The jury had already gone into recess for voting. I waved discreetly to Carla. Then, the door that led to the court's internal rooms opened and one of the men I'd seen in the hotel kitchen came out, along with six other jurors; they went back to their seats. I soon recognized the other two who had also been with Robson the night before. At the judge's request, one of them stood to read the charge. According to the jurors' vote, carried out behind closed doors, there was insufficient evidence against the defendants. *In dubio pro reo.* And that was that.

The defendants and their families embraced.

"The hat trick! Didn't I tell you?" I heard one of them say. "You going to the barbecue?" another inquired.

So this was the result of that exclusive little soirée at our hotel. A journalist I had met the day before walked past.

"I'd have been very surprised if they'd gone down," he said. "Their type always gets let off."

Txupira's mother was the only person still seated, unmoving, her eyes fixed on her feet in their old plastic sandals, which did not hide her hardened, cracked heels. Gradually, in silence, the indigenous community gathered around her, the old lady the central point upon which everyone's pain converged.

Carla remained standing at her lectern, observing the winners' jubilation. She made no attempt to hide her indignation. The day before, she had told me how hard it had been to select the jury. "It's a small town, everyone knows each other, you know how it is. They actually tried to include one of the defendants' cousins—honestly." She really felt they'd made a good selection in the end.

When at last she caught sight of me, I indicated that I'd wait for her outside and made for the courtroom door.

The now-powerful sun enveloped the city in a suffocatingly sticky, cloying heat.

A little way off, four men were trying to drag a broken old Kombi out of the road where it was blocking traffic.

"It's moving, it's moving . . ." one said.

"Push!"

"It's moving!"

"Push it!"

Then I spotted Crisântemo and the other defendants emerging from the courthouse in a single joyous group. A few journalists who'd been waiting beside me gathered around them.

"What's next? Are you pleased with the result?" one of them asked Crisântemo.

I felt a flash of electricity run through my body and shoot from my eyes as easily as bullets. The murderer fell dead to the ground. You will die, I thought, staring at him with revulsion. In the worst way possible, after appalling suffering, equal to Txupira's. I never believed in telepathy but I think he did, somehow, receive my message. I turned away, lit a cigarette, and stood waiting for Carla.

When Carla appeared, I showed her the photos on my phone of the jurors drinking with Robson. One of them grinning. Robson with his index finger raised, the center of their attention.

"Where did you take these?" she asked.

"In the hotel where I'm staying."

"When?"

"Middle of last night. I went down to the restaurant looking for water and came across this little party—at four in the morning. You can see they're drinking beer."

"Did you take these photos yourself?"

"No one saw me. But I'm pretty sure the hotel owner is suspicious. He caught me in the corridor. Today, over breakfast, he sat at my table and out of the blue he said, 'Talking is silver but silence is golden.'"

"What scum," she said. "Fucking scum. Such fucking crooked sons of bitches."

BETA

Anô queda iu ra rauê queda. There was singing and dancing to the beat of the *xuatê*, a kind of maraca made from a gourd. *Terô, terô, terô, auê.* Zapira, a tough indigenous woman from the Ch'aska community—and Marcos's mother's cousin—had given me the brew of the bitter *curimi* to drink and was now standing in the center of the *maloca*, shaking the maracas, making spiraling shapes in the air, each higher than the last, stamping her feet in time, and I was trying to follow her, focusing on that martial beat.

The women were wearing parrots' tail feathers, You're missing the rhythm, Marcos said in my ear, laughing, and glass-bead necklaces and armbands of other many-colored feathers, I laughed, too, I kept losing track, and they were singing *terô, terô, auê* and spinning in their skirts of leaves, and Marcos was laughing so hard because I couldn't get the steps right, and the men's bodies were painted with fresh urucum dye, *terô, terô,* their skin shone in the moonlight beneath masks of canvas sacking in garish colors, a simple dance but even so I couldn't get the steps right. Yellow, red, blue, they moved forward and I went back, or vice versa, everyone moved back, stepping outside the circle, and I alone went forward, out of sync with the group, as if I were forcing something out that ought to stay in, or the opposite, as if there were a clear,

65

a *perfect* line to the circle which I simply could not follow. When they started left, I'd be there pulling to the right. Let me teach you, Marcos said, handing me a gourd filled with the seeds of jungle trees—the *samaúma*, mahogany, and palm; in time, I learned all their names—and told me to shake it to the beat of my heart. I followed his advice, managed to get into line, and soon the seeds of my maraca were shaking with my heartbeat. A sense of well-being came over me, and my feet began to float.

It had been a long journey to reach the Ch'aska settlement: two hours by car to a small town on the banks of the Môa river, and from there we'd taken a motorboat another four hours. Walking through the forest, I'd been enchanted by the jungle air: so rich it seemed like a fleshy fruit, to be consumed in segments.

Before we drank the carimi, we shared some thin banana porridge and sat on palm-leaf matting around the fire. Zapira explained that the drink could open many eyes for us, not our everyday eyes that saw stones and men and animals, but other eyes, she said, eyes that saw what was hidden, what was on the other side, what was invisible, eyes that saw inside kernels, that saw into thoughts, into the sky, into the great chasm of the night, eyes that saw the dead and the spirits. My dear, you should know you will vomit, and this is good, Zapira said: We must expel everything that holds us back, all the bonds, the frustrations and blocks. My dear, will you drink carimi?

"I thought pajés were always men," I had said to Marcos, on the way.

He told me that in the past, women couldn't take part in the shamanic rituals of the Ch'aska. Their role in the community was to manage the provisions, to build fires, cook the black bean *feijão*, plant the cassavas, and make plant-fiber twine. The women told stories, gathered beads for the sacred necklaces, made maracas, and collected honey, and at first Zapira's daily rounds had been no different from that of other village women. Then, one night, she had a prophetic dream. She was visited by forest spirits who ordered her to go deep into the forest and stay there for twelve moons, eating only roots and drinking *titui*—a drink made from fermented cassava: the ritual that would prepare her to become a Ch'aska shaman. When she woke, she went straight to her father and told him. Pajés and *caciques* were consulted about Zapira's dream. Some simply laughed, some listened, others were indignant. Still others made fun of her. But Zapira was undaunted and, obeying the orders she'd received in her dream, she escaped into the forest one full-moon night, and there she stayed and ate no palm seeds or *araza*, no *tapereba* or cupuaçu, *graviola* or *jatobá* fruits, and drank not a drop of water, only a weak broth of fermented cassava and drops of the green frog's poison and carimi. When the Ch'aska men found her and tried to make her return home, she warned them that the village would be destroyed by fire if they forced her. What could they do with such obstinacy? They hauled the girl back with them and put her in the maloca along with her family. That night, a great fire blazed through the Ch'askas' crops. Horrified, the pajés and the village men met once more and were obliged to accept that having a female pajé might not be merely Zapira's mania but a genuine decision taken by the spirits, and so Zapira was sent back to the jungle. For the next twelve months, at every full moon, the pajés rubbed her with the green frog's poison, and at every seventh sun, they added more carimi to her drink. Zapira lost weight and wasted away; she almost died, and when she returned to the village, she knew better than any of them the powers of the *acapu* tree, of the *assa-peixe*, *bolbo*, *calunga*, the *sucupira*, the paracress, *losna*, *pata-de-vaca*, of everything that is leaves or bulbs or husks from the forest. "And from then on," Marcos had concluded, "she has been curing the

Ch'aska of all kinds of sickness, of worms, malaria, tuberculosis, diarrhea, and flu. She has even cured cancer."

Now I was floating through the forest; vines, spirits, herbs, shamans, Zapira, all the things Marcos had told me were floating with me, gliding, gliding around me like a flock of birds, and there were colorful winged boxes and pots, some as small as hens' eggs, others huge, so big I could have swum down into them farther than my breath would hold. But my mind stayed clear: I knew I was flying, and I knew I was dreaming; I was with the community, I, the daughter of a murdered mother, whom Amir had slapped in the face; I knew and I flew on, and then I saw that one of the pots fluttering around me had suddenly vomited a satiny fabric, printed with yellow flowers and green branches. *Torerá, ará. Arê.* When I touched it, I realized it wasn't simply a pretty piece of cloth but my mother's dressing gown that used to hang behind the bathroom door. The gown she used to wear when she'd just woken up. The same fine texture. The same sweet smell, the scent of flowers, of her perfume, of her clean body, of good soap. The smell of a dead mother. The gown flew around me and hovered over my head like an umbrella-angel. Its flower patterns came free of the fabric and tumbled down over my arms, bonding to my skin like tattoos. Something tiny broke out of the center of one of them, slid down its petals, and fell into my lap—alive. Tiny like an ant but breathing and full of life. Something I ought to love, forever. Don't leave it in the car, whispered a voice from somewhere I couldn't see. Don't lose it. Don't drop it. And I felt upset, incapable of fulfilling this responsibility. But this thing is minuscule, I thought; how could I love something so tiny? And there, I had already lost the little thing. Oh, an agony, this guilt. My sorrow. What kind of person am I—incapable of loving an ant? Losing it is as bad as killing it, the voice said. This little thing in my lap was life.

It had a pulse. How could you lose something that depended on your care? And soon the other yellow flowers were peeling away from my skin and floating off to look for what I'd lost. Like forest pigs, they snuffled at the earth, dug holes, and pulled up roots, looking for that little thing, while the voice said: You may not forget. Forgetting is losing, and losing is killing. Once more they brought me the miniature burden I had to carry. But I was spinning through the sky, reckless and distracted, and oops, I lost the little creature again. Look there it is, rising on the swell. Forgetting is losing, the voice said again. Losing is killing. Finding is living. Look for the creature, the voice said, find that tiny thing this very minute because it—this living, breathing thing that you have lost, it is your mother.

I didn't tell Marcos any of this when we got back. We made the return boat trip in silence.

Later, in the car, with my feet resting on the dashboard, my whole body exhausted after the long night, I decided that my delirium must have come from so deeply wanting, dreaming, daring to believe that the machine of my memory could be made to work once more. Even having believed all my life that it was a blessing I couldn't remember. A blessing and a life sentence. I had always hoped that one day, something, a treatment, an event, a crack on the head—something would reactivate my memory and I'd be able to recall everything I had seen the night my father killed my mother. In all the detail I'd recounted to my grandmother at the time. It was only because of me that they knew it had not been an accident. If this was inside me, I had to remember. In the end, I think, this was what I'd been seeking with Zapira: my buried memory.

Before we arrived back in Cruzeiro do Sul, Marcos told me that people in the city were asking about me.

"Which people?" I asked.

"The people here," he said. "They're wondering if you're a journalist."

"A journalist?"

"Yes. They say you're writing about shady deals we're doing. About the city's shady dealing. That's what they're saying."

IT WAS ALCEU WHO KILLED EUDINÉIA & Heroilson who killed Iza & Wendeson who killed Regina & Marcelo who killed Soraia & Ermício who killed Silvana & Creso who killed Chirley & still more, Degmar was killed by Ádila & Ketlen was killed by Henrique & Rusyleid was killed by Tadeu & Juciele was killed by Itaan & Qucila was killed by Roni & Jaqueline was killed by Sinval & Daniela was killed by Alberto & Raele was killed by Geraldo and none of these crimes, which happened seven, ten, twelve years ago, took any more than three hours of a court's time.

Regina annoyed Wendeson, she used to break his concentration with the crap she had on the radio & Ermício found a photo of Silvana on her phone wearing a bikini & Daniela wanted to split up with Alberto & Rusyleid wanted to take a break from Tadeu & Degmar had already asked Ádila for a divorce & Iza died, actually, because she refused to channel funds into Heroilson's cachaça. That's what Iza was like, Heroilson told the judge—a complicated woman, difficult even. Do you know who Silvana sent that photo to, of herself in her bikini? To a colleague at her office. I let Silvana work and she did this to me, Ermício testified. In her bikini! Turn down that fucking radio, Wendeson had warned a thousand times. But who says Regina ever obeyed?

Ermício & Henrique & Heroilson were drunk at the time of their crimes. The problem, one said, was that her rudeness got too mixed up with my cachaça. That was the problem. Queila died because she got a promotion, from clerk to the clerks' manager. She thought she was all that, her murderer said. And Sinval asked Jaqueline, in tears: did you screw that guy, Jaque? To which his victim replied: yes, I screwed him all night, Sinval, he isn't a dickless wonder like you, he's got a job, Sinval, he has a big dick and he's a driver & one crucial detail: Tadeu acted in self-defense, this must be pointed out. In legitimate self-defense, Tadeu cut off Rusyleid's head.

The conclusion I reached by my second week in court was this: we women are dying like flies. You men get hammered and kill us. Men want to fuck and kill us. Men get enraged and kill us. Men want a bit of fun and kill us. Men discover our lovers and kill us. We leave them and men kill us. Men get another lover and kill us. Men are taken down a peg and kill us. Men get home tired after work and kill us.

And, in court, everyone says the fault is ours. We women know how to provoke. We know how to make life hell, how to wreck a guy's life. We are disloyal and vindictive—it's our fault. We are the trigger. Really, what *are* we doing here, at this party, at this time, in these clothes? Really, why did we accept the drink we were offered? Worse still, why didn't we refuse the invitation to go up to that hotel room with that brute if we didn't want to fuck? Well, now we've been warned. Don't leave the house, certainly not at night. Don't get drunk. Don't be independent. Don't go this way, or that way. Don't work. Don't choose that skirt or that neckline. But whoever said we follow the rules? We wear miniskirts. Necklines down to our belly buttons. Shorts that barely hang on by our bum-cracks. We go too far. We go down dark alleys. We keep our pussies charged up and ready to go. We draw conclusions. We work all day. We're independent. We have lovers. We giggle loudly. We support the household. We let it all go to shit. The strange thing is we don't kill. It's incredible how rarely we kill. Given the stats on how many of us are dying, we ought to be killing more often. But, due to some problem that could be glandular or could be structural, possibly ethical or possibly physical, we prefer not to kill. That's how it is; we generally end up tossed onto waste ground, like Chirley. For defiance. We are chopped up and buried, like Ketlen, in the yard. For disobedience.

You could have filled a stadium, one of those really big ones, with the fathers and mothers and sisters and brothers and daughters and sons and cousins and friends who came to the courthouse to grieve the deaths of these women. In the hot sun, amid the storms, I saw them arrive in groups, all as crushed as the people from Txupira's village. I was miserable for them. I took photos of a few. Rusyleid's mother was as pretty as her murdered daughter. "Do you want to see my girl?" she asked, and showed me Rusyleid smiling in a 3 x 4 photo that had grown so worn it had the velvety texture of old paper money.

This is Rusyleid: lighthearted, hard-working, a good girl, never in trouble with anyone, I don't understand why they killed my little girl. Silvana's son, Cauã, who was six months old when she died, already knew how to read and write, his grandmother told me. "Since he started going to school, he's been calling me his mother. I think it's because of the other children. He wants to have a mother, too." I thought of taking these photos back to show my boss. To show her the sweet little face of Cauã who still cries and misses his mother. But dead women's children have no value in Denise's book of statistics. So I stuck them into my notebook where the dead women were piling higher every day. The women from the court cases as well as those I fished from the papers. Already my notebook was overflowing with murdered women and I still had another week of work to go.

During that time, there were two longer hearings with white defendants and their own private defense teams. Both were acquitted. Dalton and Reinaldo got away with it. One was a businessman, the other a dentist. One rich, the other a millionaire—they walked free. When I mentioned this to the state's defending counsel, he said: "That's standard for crimes in Brazil these days. We're just putting Black people and the poor away for longer and longer."

The dentist murderer had injured his right arm with the knife he'd used to kill his wife. Before he appeared in front of the judge with his eye-wateringly expensive lawyers, there was some complication with his condition and he ended up losing his arm. The jury decided for that reason and that alone, he'd already been punished enough. A dentist without a right arm is like a singer without a voice. A storyteller without a tongue. A footballer without a foot. The homicidal dentist left his trial by the front door, smiling, with his new lover hanging off his bionic arm.

The other defendant, despite being found guilty by the jury, enjoyed a similar fate. Given that he was responsible for the distribution of chilled drinks across the state and a major patron of the city's cultural life, a first-time offender and a good father, the judge gave him a one-year prison sentence. One year! But with probation granted on the spot, this murderer also left by the front door.

In nine of the fourteen cases, the victims knew their executioners. Six were killed by their husbands, two by their boyfriends, one by a neighbor. Some had already filed formal complaints. This too was part of my work: to evaluate the statistics. Only Raele, the clerk, didn't know her attacker.

"You seem surprised," Carla later remarked. "Type 'killed by' into Google and see what you get."

Later, I tried it.

"Killed by":

Killed by her boyfriend

Killed by her husband

Killed by her ex

Killed by her partner

Killed by her father

Killed by her father-in-law . . .

The problem with discovering this kind of thing is that you get addicted. Every day I'd type in "killed by" and get that tide of blood head-on. It doesn't matter where you are or what social class you belong to and it doesn't matter what you do for a living. It's dangerous being a woman.

That week, over dinner, Carla advised me to take a bit more care. She described how, out of the blue, her brother had begun to have vomiting episodes. "He was waking up in the middle of the night to be sick," she said. "He was eating normally, his appetite was normal. But he was vomiting. He seemed fine, he could drive or do whatever he wanted, but then suddenly he'd have to stop everything and throw up. In the morning, in the evening, any time of day or night. You know how it is with Italian families: my mother went into a complete tailspin. She took him for an endoscopy and all kinds of tests, which showed nothing at all. It was a long time before we connected his vomiting with the anatomy course he was taking at medical school. He himself didn't see the link. Actually, he was having the time of his life cutting up bodies with scalpels. Opening up their skulls. Poking around in the intestines and livers. Outwardly he was loving it. Inside, he was freaking out. So he'd got into this cycle I call vomiting death. In a different way," Carla went on, "I also had my death-vomiting phase, when I started working on the cases of all these murdered women. Because it's really something, this Fordist production line. Women are dying on an industrial scale. Except, instead of vomiting like my brother, I couldn't handle relationships with men anymore. For me, men turned into something of an enemy, you know? Now, after a long time, I'm in a sort of test-drive phase. I test out one, then another. Always taking it very slow. Always with a trusty thick stick on my side of the bed. Say the guy brings his toothbrush to my place, that triggers my red alert. Take Paulo, for example: he's a sweetheart. Really a lovely guy. But I never let him stay more than two nights a week at mine. It's my golden rule. Better safe than sorry."

I liked Carla. After the hearings, we always went for a drink or a swim in one of the creeks. We would lie in the sun and talk through the trials. I admired her intelligence and especially her seriousness. I never showed her my scrapbook of never-ending female bodies. Perhaps she would have thought it another kind of death-vomiting. Perhaps she'd have had a point. In a way, collecting cases is not all that different from nausea.

And, apparently, my notebook was the only place you could really see the scale of murdered women. I couldn't find one line on the subject in the press. Nothing about Chirley, Queila, or Daniela. The only case that interested the journalists was Txupira's. Not because they had any feeling for Txupira or any real sense of the tragedy of her death at only fourteen. They couldn't have cared less about her. She wasn't white. She didn't fit the category of victims the press likes to investigate. Worst of all, she was indigenous. In our particular caste system which keeps the rich and white at the top, indigenous people are lower than Black people, who are lower than the poor, who are lower even than women. In our caste system, the lives of the indigenous people have the same value as the lives of the certified mad and the children who beg at traffic lights. We treat our indigenous peoples like shit. What the papers really like is murderers. Especially when they are white and rich, like Crisântemo. Or at least middle-class and white. We treat these men like film stars.

In a way, I felt partly responsible for the success of Crisântemo and his accomplices.

On Carla's suggestion, the night before Marcos and I left Cruzeiro do Sul to drink the carimi tea with the Ch'aska, I had been to see editors at the local paper, the *Diário da Estrela.* "Look for Rita, the editor-in-chief," she'd said. "Show her your photos and tell her what you told me."

Carla had appealed the jury's decision and requested a judicial review of Txupira's case, based on the discovery of new evidence: my photos. As part of the appeal, aside from disbanding the jury, she intended to request preventive imprisonment of the defendants. "We're in for another two, maybe three years of struggle, at least, and hoo-ha in the press is the only way to speed things up," she said.

Rita greeted me in a tank top, cowboy boots, and a long, flowing, brightly colored skirt. I warmed to her direct manner and her bearing, which spoke of energy and efficiency.

Our meeting was brief. She examined the photo, then announced buoyantly, "This won't be measly picayune, that's all I can say for now."

"Picayune?"

She laughed.

"Trivial. Small beer, in localese. You need to learn the Acre lingo. You want my advice?" she asked. "Take the back door. This time of day, the whole city already knows you're here."

Three days later, the upshot of my visit was printed nice and big on the *Diário da Estrela*'s front page. "They did it," accused the headline in tall capitals. Photos of Crisântemo Alves, Abelardo Ribeiro Maciel, and Antônio Francisco Medeiros showed the boys in their playboy element: surfing, emerging from nightclubs, climbing into speedboats, riding motorbikes, and driving luxury cars, accompanied in every shot by their respective babes. But the photo that led the story was one I'd taken of the lawyer, Robson, and the jurors in the hotel kitchen.

The article pulled no punches. It correctly accused the defense of breaking the principle of jury isolation, but it made the mistake of offering its own verdict, labelling the defendants the guilty parties, even before the retrial.

"The owner of the paper is a political enemy of the Alves family," Carla explained. "I'm just taking advantage of that."

Unfortunately, the effect was the opposite of what we were after. There was no public outcry. No one took to the streets demanding justice for Txupira or chanting "Txupira—present!" What happened was a reaction against the paper. The city simply closed ranks on the side of the murderers. Poor boys, they said. Lynched by the media. Look at this country we live in, they said. The law acquits but the media condemns. They said: In this country, you can't even share a beer among friends without being accused of criminal association.

José was one of the first to side with Txupira's murderers. He also decided that I alone could have taken that photo.

The same day the article was published, Zenóbio came to

see me, visibly embarrassed, to say I would have to leave my room because "the hotel was full."

"Only if you mean full of mosquitoes," I replied.

Carla chuckled when I told her. I stayed with her for two nights, until I was able to rent the home of her friend Lena, a family lawyer born and brought up in Cruzeiro do Sul who was attending a course in São Paulo. "You can use my car, too," Lena said, on the phone. "Please make use of everything. As long as you can collect my dog from my mother and give him some TLC."

Lena's house was welcoming, full of color, and crammed with indigenous objects—bows, arrows, and headdresses, mostly. It also had a garden that felt like a forest, with the bonus of being a little way out of the city. Oto, a mutt with a black stripe across his eyes that looked like a pair of wraparound shades, and I got on very well, and every morning, before I went to the courthouse, we would go for a long walk in the forest. Only then did I begin to understand Marcos's joke about Acre. "We don't have precious ores or gems, we're just a vegetal entity in the fourth state of matter: not solid, liquid, or gas, but Acre." During our walks, I came to the conclusion that his fourth state of matter was a combination of plant solids with plant gases. You could sniff the air as if it were dough, softly solid, a compact mass of oxygen, too dense to be considered gaseous, with an aroma of moss, earth, flowers, foliage, dung, chili peppers, rotting wood, animals, and breeze fresher than any I'd experienced before and which lingered in the mouth for hours, like the flavor of an excellent wine.

I felt so good in this climate, with the natural world around me, the scents of the foliage, that I found myself making peace with my grandmother. "I've been thinking," she called to say, "now that you're better settled out there, isn't this my opportunity to see the sights of Acre?" That was my grandma Yolanda all over. You give her a hand, and before you know it, she's taken your foot, too.

The following Saturday, Carla, Paulo, Marcos, and I went swimming in the creek close to my new house.

That night, I cooked a fish for them, one Marcos had caught the day before. I baked it with onions, coarse salt, and potatoes. Marcos prepared a side of *farofa* the local, indigenous way using his mother's recipe, and we had cupuaçu ice cream, bought earlier in the city, for dessert.

It was a special night. It had been a good while since I'd felt so relaxed. The house was practically my own and I felt I belonged in Acre. After dinner, as we sat around on the veranda—the wine may have played a part here—everyone began telling their life stories, their toughest times. Marcos loved his mother and said he had some issues with his father. "Idiot Indian" was his father's name for his mother, before they separated. His mother had taken Marcos to her community after the divorce. But his father had brought the police there with him to fetch Marcos back. "I only became close to my mother again fifteen years later," Marcos said. "It took me a long time to feel proud of her, to understand she isn't stupid."

Carla adored her parents. "I love them—far from where I am! My family is a blender that's always on. We're a thick soup, all whizzed up together. I had to run away to Acre so I could live my own life."

"Normal," was Paulo's response when it was his turn. "Normal father, normal mother: nothing to say."

I think that's what made me say it. "My mother was killed by my father when I was four. I saw it all, but I don't remember."

All three of them stared at me, the way the society for animal protection looks at a street dog that's been stoned to death. And that was the end of the life-stories show-and-tell. Later that night I caught a few sidelong looks with thoughtful expressions: *Your father murdered your mother?* But no one had the courage to ask me more about it.

Luckily Paulo had brought some marijuana and, once we'd smoked a little, the tension eased and we laughed at the stories he and Marcos told about the local jungle.

"Here," Paulo said, "a guy's gotta learn quick how to tell a monkey's chatter from a leopard's roar." He described frogs the size of steer, spiders with fifteen-centimeter legs, and seven-meter-long snakes that were "highly timid." Carla burst into giggles at the phrase, and Paulo wanted to know why he couldn't describe a creature as "highly timid" when we always talk about things being "highly dangerous."

"I'm not saying you can't say it. It's just very funny!"

Paulo stayed quiet for the rest of the night. He only spoke up again when the conversation turned to Txupira and I said I wished Txupira's murderers would die of ass-cancer.

"That wouldn't be too hard to arrange," he said. "This is the heartland of the hired killer. It wouldn't cost more than a thousand reais to contract some *bugreiro* to eliminate those kids."

"Didn't you hear what she said?" Carla asked. "She doesn't want them to die any old how. It has to be cancer."

"Ass-cancer," Marcos added.

And we fell about laughing.

I slept with Marcos that night. It was the first time I'd had sex with anyone since the slap. It would have been great had he not said afterwards that he wanted me to have his children. I giggled, petrified. Something tiny to love and not lose—that's all I need, I thought.

In the early hours, Carla called.

"They've found Rita's body," she said.

It took a moment for me to work this out.

"Rita," she repeated. "The editor of the paper that reported on Txupira's murderers. She's been killed."

7

KILLED BY HER BROTHER-IN-LAW

When the police arrived, Alessandra Fernandes Silva's
four-year-old daughter warned them:
"My mother is deaded in there."
The child, who witnessed the crime and spent
part of the night
sitting beside her mother's body,
also informed the police that
the murderer was her own uncle.

J

I FEEL TREMBLY, I'M GETTING SWEATS, dizziness, other strange effects. I know what's going on.

I pointed to the tattoo. There inside the casket was a horrible paradox: the word "dreams" along Rita's right instep. Her body was surrounded by a bed of flowers.

"I've never seen Rita without her boots," Carla said.

"Her tattoo," I said.

"What about it?"

"It's awful to see the word 'dreams' tattooed on a dead girl's foot."

But she didn't hear my answer. She had walked over to meet Denis, Rita's twin brother, who had just arrived at the service with their parents.

Abstinence syndrome.

Almost a week earlier, late on the previous Saturday night after dining at my house, Carla had spotted a message from Rita on her cell phone. The women had not been close but had admired each other professionally and spoken often, especially after Rita's paper had published the piece about Txupira's murderers.

Denis had found Rita's body only forty minutes after that message on Carla's phone. An agronomist who lived in Rio Branco, Denis came to Cruzeiro do Sul—usually by car because he hated flying—to visit clients' farms in the area, and these trips happened often enough that Rita had given him a copy of her house key. The twins were close, speaking almost daily on the phone and going for runs together on the earthen footpaths around the community. Early that morning, Denis had been disturbed to find his sister's house unlocked. It was blowing a gale then, and in regions where gales regularly uproot trees and tear off roofs, the people tend to take extra care. When he entered the living room, Denis saw Rita's body slumped on the floor at the foot of the stairs.

I need your loving enzymes and hysterical acids running down my glucose chargers.

A few hours later, I arrived at Carla's house and found her devastated. She had just been speaking to Denis.

"Listen to this," she said, pressing her phone to my ear. "*Hi Carla, Rita here. I know it's late but I've got some info that you'll want to hear. Call me when you get up.*"

Carla told me that she'd hardly been able to wait for dawn before calling Rita, but when she did, Denis had answered the phone.

Before we even reached Rita's house on that ill-fated morning, Carla was convinced that Rita's death could not have been caused by an accident on the stairs, as Denis, despite his bewilderment, said the police had suggested. Rita had been young, athletic, even muscular. It was hard to imagine her toppling down the stairs like a sack of potatoes without even trying to hang on to the banister or protect her head.

"It wasn't an accident," Carla said over and over as we drove to Rita's house. "Certainly not after Rita published that article."

Grounded by the evidence of my photos, and despite local support for the three murderers, the article had spread like a virus to other newspapers and websites, and now there was state-level pressure for Txupira's case to be retried. "It's straightforward logic," Carla said. "The boys belong to major families who've been in charge ever since Acre was annexed to Brazil. They're used to fixing problems with their guns."

Of course Carla felt guilty, even though she knew that Rita would have published the article with or without her help and my photos. Rita was well known for her bravery; she, too, shot from the hip.

Later, when we read the official report, we learned that the police had quite a different story about what had happened to Rita. For them, there had been no signs of forced entry or burglary. They had found no signs of a fight, either. An empty bottle of red wine on the dining table was the only thing that had attracted the officers' attention. "She was probably drunk," the investigator told Denis.

I had spent the past few weeks reading judicial reports on the crimes logged with our task force, and it seemed to me that the problem of impunity began with the forensic investigation. The investigators would arrive at a crime scene however they were able, in dented old bangers or on foot, without equipment or the necessary kit for their investigation, still unpaid for previous jobs, racing off to answer other calls, to look into more corpses waiting for them elsewhere—and especially on the weekends. They would give the victim a onceover, a cursory top-to-bottom and *finito*, job done.

In less scientific language, I need your legs wrapped around mine. I love you. Amir. PS: I won't give up.

Carla had persuaded Denis to contract a private criminal investigator. At the funeral, he told us he was meeting with the investigator on Monday and hoped there would be more information about his sister's death. I could see that he and Carla wanted to speak alone, so I left them and went outside to smoke.

It had rained heavily that morning and the whole square was a patchwork of puddles. I sat on the low wall enclosing the garden, lit a cigarette, and read Amir's latest message to me from start to finish. *I feel trembly, I'm getting the sweats, dizziness, other strange effects. I know what's going on. Abstinence syndrome. I need your loving enzymes and hysterical acids running down my glucose chargers. In less scientific language, I need your legs wrapped around mine. I love you. Amir. PS: I won't give up.*

Hysterical acids. We'd had a good laugh together, Amir and I, I thought. I remembered being in bed with him, spent and breathless after making love. "You are knackering my cock," he'd say. I'd felt so happy about our sex life. I read the text through again and again. It was the kind of message I deeply wanted to believe. My fingers itched. All I had to do was touch my index to the telephone icon beside the message.

Hi, Amir, I'm missing you too. I miss your sense of humor. Your intelligence. I loved fucking you, Amir. I loved talking to you. I loved spending Sundays in bed, my head on your chest, watching American series on TV. Such a nice life; why would I make things difficult?

I was angry with myself for letting these thoughts through. After all, it was the third and final week of our task force. What further evidence did I need of the type of man who slaps a woman in the face? The type that considers an emotional relationship a kind of license to kill. The type who believes that taking the trash out is the best he can do for you. You with your eight-hour work days, cleaning, sorting, scrubbing, driving, operating, educating, doing everything under the sun. You who've already cooked, cleaned, ironed, and got the kids into bed. I had seen all of this at the courthouse. Before the slap, verbal abuse: tramp, lazy slut, whore. That's how it was for Helena. Same for Marta. Shut your mouth, you tart. You slag. You cow. The slap is a watershed moment. It initiates the beating-up phase. The shoves, punches, every kind of hitting. That's how it was for Rayna. Knocked to the floor as if it were still the stone age. Some women, like Lindalva, are deafened before they die. Some men rupture the eardrums of the women they called darling, my love, my princess, hot stuff. Of course, a man can break your arm even before the insults begin. Some are desperate, a touch reckless. They want to have the last word as soon as possible. But it's clear that the way you'll die depends on several factors. The male's alcohol intake. His degree of general frustration. The pressure he's under at work.

And if you laugh in his face, things may happen at a dizzying pace—never forget this point. Kicks can also play a part. Kicks to the belly, the legs, the face, once you're on the floor. To teach you, they say. To warn you: If you leave me now, I'll do you in. I'll kill your parents, kill our kids. And when they're bored of hitting you with their hands and feet they pick up the pressure cooker, the knife, the vacuum cleaner or some other solid, heavy, or pointed object, anything that burns, pierces, or constricts, anything to put a stop to the lives of their girlfriends, wives, partners, lovers. I saw it with my own eyes: the statements, police reports, photos, videos, security camera footage. The evidence was overwhelming.

But don't go thinking that it all happens in one go. No, they proceed in parts: one thing, then another. First they subdue us. Then they beat us. After that, they kill us. I saw the photos, heard the statements, read the police reports. Marciane's mouth was slit from ear to ear with a razor blade. Because she'd reported her husband to the police after he beat her up. "Go back there and fix this shit you've created," he said to her. For Magali, before the killing, before beating, before pummelling, and even before the very first slap, Wevi was a prince—like Amir. At least, that's what Magali's mother told the court. "I've met a prince," Magali had said; in fact, she'd met her future murderer. I myself had told my grandmother that Amir was an aristocrat. And Raul—Raul even knelt in the middle of the street before Lívia, to apologize for breaking her right arm and beg her to come back. "I'll never break another bone in your body," he said. Lívia accepted his pleas. Then she got pregnant. "She was my whole life," Raul said, crying, after he killed her. He got ten years.

I heard it all. In the plenary, they all say the same thing. Milton & Rondiney & Edson & Nildo & Ricardo & Ítalo & Rodrigo & Fares & Brayan. Sexual problems. Drinking problems. Adultery. Some of them come to court with their psychiatrists, pleading mental unfitness. I can't remember anything, they say. Have pity on me, they argue: I'm epileptic. I'm the worst expression of bipolar. I'm schizophrenic. But the truth is most of them are completely typical, just as they are completely murderous. Children, poverty, unemployment, drinking—none of these is the real problem. They kill because they like killing women, just as they like fishing or playing football.

Of course they aren't born like this. Only a few are born to murder. But psychopaths are an elite class of murderer. The general working mass of murderers, the majority of them, I'd say, have to learn to hate before they can kill. My father was a good student. But there's nothing easier than learning to hate women. There is no shortage of teachers. Fathers teach it, the state teaches it, the legal system teaches it, the market teaches it, and culture, and propaganda. But the best teacher, according to my colleague Bia, is pornography.

Women-killers, I discovered, have their own vocabulary. You have to know how to translate what they're saying when they say "I love you." When they say "I love you," they mean "You've met your master." When they say they feel jealous, they're referring to the right to use their own property. He is overseer of this plantation. He's the rancher; you're the cattle. He's the owner and you are the product, like his car, his phone, his house, or his shoe. And your marriage, your love, your bond are your fatal indictment. When he begs forgiveness, when he begs to come back, he is warning you: Your countdown has begun. Now you'd best watch out. Get away from this man. Disappear. Delete the message.

After deleting mine, I went back in to the memorial service, thinking that Amir was not in torment due to love, as he wanted me to think. All he wanted was somehow to get me back so he could then kill me. But I'd promised myself this, at least: I was not going to die like my mother. No fucking way.

At the door, I bumped into Carla and Denis.

"We're getting coffee," Carla said. "Come too?"

From the bar, I could see goats grazing in what looked to be an abandoned construction site. It was disturbing, simply sitting beside Denis, hearing his voice; he was so very like Rita. The same skin tone, the same eyes, the same mouth and smile, the same expressions, the same build. It was as though Rita were right here, in drag, playing a strange trick on us.

"Look in her drawers," Carla was saying, "on her computer, in her wardrobe. It has to be somewhere."

"If I only knew where to begin," Denis said.

"You heard the voicemail. She herself said it was a lead. It could be, I don't know, in an envelope, on a pen drive."

Denis was beginning to show the strain. He told us how, the day before, he'd given his statement to the police but it had been ridiculous.

"They made me hand over my gas receipts from the journey," he said. "But it was the way they asked me: 'Where were you at the time your sister died?'"

Carla said, "It's all play-acting. If they actually suspected anything, they would be investigating you."

As we parted ways, Carla and I agreed to meet up later, at the courthouse, for the conclusion of our task force.

"Take care," she said.

"Are you afraid?" I asked.

"They killed Rita, so they could kill us, too."

"You won't even consider the theory of an accident?"

"It wasn't an accident. You yourself took those photos. Think about it."

"They're not going to knock me off in broad daylight. That would be stupid of them."

"They're stupid. Killing Rita is proof of their stupidity."

I went back to the house, picking up cherry tomatoes at the local grocery on the way back. I opened a tin of black olives and put a dish of pasta together. After that, I went for a stroll with Oto in the forest. It was my last working day here, and I still hadn't booked my return flight or packed my suitcases. Not even thought about it. Marcos called to ask if I'd like to go with him to see the Ch'aska.

In court that afternoon, apart from myself, there were only the mother and sister of Scarlath, a 26-year-old Black girl from whom a tire-dealer named Fares had borrowed ten reais. Scarlath's suffering had begun the day she went to get her loan back. Fares took two whole days to kill her, and he did a real butcher's job, too, cutting off her legs first, then her arms, then her head, then her breasts and vagina. He filmed it all. Fares's workshop was plastered with years' worth of calendars of gorgeous women, all naked, showing their breasts, pussies, asses, squatting, legs spread, mouths open, perfect teeth biting perfect lips, eyes all come-eat-me-out. It seemed Fares liked to do target practice on them. He'd take aim at a breast, a butt, an asshole, and throw darts at it. He'd finish by using a screwdriver to pierce the pretty women's eyes. The calendars were full of holes. Fares's phone was full of porn videos.

I sent everything to Bia in our São Paulo office, because it was her task to catalogue the crimes that involved women's dismemberment, mutilation, and disembowelment for the book Denise was writing.

I couldn't face listening to the defending counsel. I know she was only doing her job, providing a full defense case, but you get tired of hearing that kind of insinuation, as if Scarlath, being a prostitute, deserved her fate. By a decision of four to three, the jury sent Fares to prison. For eighteen years, the judge decreed.

As we left the court, I went to speak with Scarlath's mother.

"My mother was murdered by my father," I said.

I couldn't believe I'd said it aloud—I'd held out my hand to her and the words surged out like vomit. For years, I'd held them deep inside me, tucked away at the back of a drawer padlocked with seven locks. Then they burst from my mouth as if from some completely independent mechanism. Look at you now, I thought.

"My daughter is not a prostitute," Scarlath's mother said simply.

"I know," I replied, but she had already turned away and was shuffling toward the bus stop.

Marcos and I were on our way to the Ch'aska village when Bia called from the office, reeling from the impact of the material I'd sent over.

"Those bloody hardcore feminists are right," she said. "Where do these fuckers learn to do this shit to us? In the porn lessons they get from day one of life." Bia was deep in the case notes and no one could staunch her flow when the topic was pornography. She loved to explain, in her best headteacher style, her gleanings from books on the subject: that porn had been created "by the same guys who used to burn witches. When the fun was over with witches and all those fireworks, they invented another way of killing women—porn. See?"

"Pornography," she would say, "is fundamentally a factory for women-killers. The guys spend their whole lives seeing this or that dumb tart, seeing other guys locking down those pussies, other guys cracking the whip over our backsides, and they end up thinking it's normal to throttle their own wife when they're out of sorts."

But Bia hadn't called just to give me a history lesson. She wanted to know if I was on the way back to São Paulo.

My work was done. Our task force had wrapped up. There was nothing to keep me in Acre.

"What time's your flight? Denise wants to schedule a meeting on Monday, first thing. Can I confirm it?"

I said yes, I'd be back in São Paulo before Monday.

That's what I said. I sighed and said I'd go back, but I didn't.

GAMMA

A bouquet of shoots, organisms, of rain just passed over; of fruit skins and rosewood, of creepers, pollen, and living animals; of petals, dry leaves, resin, decaying roots, of burned foliage, dead animals, flowers, and soil, of honey, myrrh, and dung; of *cumaru* oil and crabwood, of chili peppers that could make you cry. I read somewhere that the forest holds the smell of beginnings, of dust, brine, and oxygen, the smell of single-celled life, of cells reproducing, of molecules multiplying, a smell of potency and slime.

I saw something glowing in there. A luminous point at the heart of the wilderness. And here as I walked, I listened to the crackling, huffing sounds of my footsteps on the turf as I walked on into the dimness. I walked and walked until I could see torch flames just ahead, and a sound of water, too, leading me forward.

Upon emerging from the dense forest, I found them. The moon was rising and they were waiting for me, I saw that straight away. They were gathered around a small lake. All I could see of some was their long, thick hair flowing in cascades over their bodies, over their genitals, down to their feet. White women, Black women, transparent women, mahogany women, blue and light brown and yellow, women of every color, but I would only notice this when we marched into our first battle. What I saw now was how strong and how many they were.

"You took your time," one of them whispered.

Another one handed me a bow and arrows. "Take these," she said. Then I saw that the women were holding not ornamental torches but weapons of war, which glinted in the moonlight. Many had cut off one breast in order to better bear the spears they carried close to their bodies. Others had chosen to bind their breasts with strips of cloth. Still others left theirs loose: some small and budding, some wrinkled, some vast or sagging low, some pointing out into the world, some asymmetrical, some drop-shaped or rounded.

"You don't need clothes here," said a third woman, unbuttoning my dress.

Naked, I joined them around the lake which, in the moonlight, looked like a great silver-plated pond.

Absolutely nothing surprised me—that was the shock: my familiarity with these women and this ritual, my ease with the bow and arrows. It was as if I'd come home to a place I'd never been but never ought to have left. This was my tribe. Taking up my arms, I followed them into the lake for the purification ritual, chanting our summons to the Lady of the Green Stones.

Now she rose out of the water like a Venus, as naked as we were, with long hair like almost all of us, carrying a basket filled with soft green things of different sizes, none larger than an egg. As each of us picked one up, it turned into a little jade nugget. Mine bore a simple image of a key.

Later, when we sat down around our Lady of the Green Stones, she asked me about the key's significance. I couldn't think of anything.

Then she asked, "Do you bring news?"

I nodded. I knew what this meant.

"Say their names," she urged.

"They killed Txupira. They killed Queila. They killed Daniela. They killed Eudinéia & Iza & Silvana & Degmar & Raele. They killed Juciele. They killed Regina."

As each name was spoken, the women warriors around me hissed and growled, as if they were sharpening knives.

"They killed Scarlath. They killed Tatiana Spitzner. They killed Elaine Figueiredo Lacerda. They killed Rayane Barros de Castro. They killed Fernanda Siqueira. They killed Rita, the journalist. There are many names missing," I said. "I haven't read today's papers."

"Were these isolated instances?" asked the Lady of the Green Stones.

"No," I said. "There is a pattern to the killings."

"Then it is a war," she replied.

"An epidemic," added a pregnant woman.

"They kill and we are dying," I said.

"They are our enemies," another said.

"They only come here when they want to procreate," the pregnant one swore.

Another: "We hunt them in these parts—and play with their little peckers."

"Mine had a big cock," the pregnant one said.

They all laughed.

"What if there are boy babies?" I asked.

"We don't want men. Not here," explained the tallest woman. "They kill rivers and forests."

"They know how to fuck a lady," another said, licking her lips.

"What if your kid is a boy?" I asked the pregnant one.

Another: "They kill women, they kill kids, and they're killing the oceans."

"It will be a girl," the pregnant one answered.

"We have to start with someone," said the Lady of the Green Stones.

"But what if it is a boy?" I asked again.

"We'll take the boys to their fathers to bring up, on their own territory. If they don't want them, we'll kill father and son," the pregnant one replied, stroking her huge belly.

"I don't want to kill children," I said.

"These aren't ordinary children. They're men. They become men."

"We raise our children with infinite love," the pregnant woman persisted.

"We raise our daughters with great courage," another said. "To live full lives and destroy their enemies."

The tallest woman again: "We kill males."

One by one, the others joined the chorus.

"We kill them and eat them."

"Roasted."

"Not all of them. Some aren't even good enough to eat."

"They're rotten."

"Full of toxins."

"I like men. Or rather, I like the idea of them, not the things themselves."

"The idea of them was nice enough. But it didn't work out."

"I like decent men—at a distance. Men at a good distance—from me."

"Roast men aren't half bad."

"I prefer armadillo meat."

"They like to bear arms."

A North American woman: "They like grabbing women by the pussy."

"They like raping."

"And war-mongering."

"And pornography. Misogynistic porn."

"My friend Bia says that porn is killing us," I said.

Another assured me Bia was right. "Pornography is a long lesson in how to despise, humiliate, and kill women."

"But we're no puritans."

"Our pussies are fully wired."

"Electric pussies."

"Men are bullshit."

"They like beating us up. They like to harass us."

"They like to tear us to pieces. They enjoy rape."

"They stick bits of bottles or sharp things into our vaginas."

"Impaling us."

"They do killing on credit."

"They kill dogs and they kill forests. They kill rivers and they kill women. Not in that order."

"Some men are tasty. With yam, or farofa."

I said: "My father killed my mother."

Everyone looked at me.

"Yet another one motherless," I heard one whisper.

The Lady of the Green Stones called for silence. "With whom shall we begin?"

"Crisântemo," I said.

And the chorus chanted: "Death to Crisântemo!"

The Lady of the Green Stones: "We need some criteria. Some kind of order."

"He murdered Txupira," I said. "And Rita, the journalist. He wasn't alone—Abelardo Ribeiro Maciel and Antônio Francisco Medeiros played their parts in both crimes. But we can kill those two afterwards."

"But what about your father? Don't you want to begin with your father?"

"He's already dead," I said.

"We can bring him back. We have that power." The Lady of the Green Stones pointed at the jade nugget in my lap.

"What would I do with my father?" I asked, confused.

"You could kill him. With your own hands."

"I'd prefer to kill men who are still alive. There are so many. Alceu & Heroilson & Wendeson & Tadeu & Alberto & Geraldo & Sinval & Dalton & Reinaldo . . . "

Our Lady nodded. "Better we begin with the ones who got away with it in court. Those who were judged and cleared despite their guilt."

"I would start with Crisântemo," I said again.

"Do all agree?" asked the Lady of the Green Stones.

Spears rose and fists flew up.

The single chant rang out: "Death to Crisântemo! Death to Crisântemo!"

I said, "I have a plan to trap him."

"Witchcraft?" asked the giggly one.

"A few of us could hide in the waste plot on Rua Rui Barbosa, a dark and isolated little street he has to take on his way home," I said. "There's no CCTV and no neighbors there. I've been observing his daily routine. He gets up late. He says he's studying but it's not true. He claims he's working on his father's land but he spends most of his time in front of the computer, surfing and posting crap. Friday nights he goes out to a club. He gets home late, always plastered. That's when we'll get him. We'll leave a car in the middle of the road. We'll use our asses and tits as lures. 'Our tire burst,' we'll say . . . " Suddenly the drink's bitter taste flooded my mouth.

"Take her out among the trees," the Lady of the Green Stones ordered.

I closed my eyes, woozy. My heart was racing.

"Bend over," Marcos said.

I vomited a yellow liquid that smelled of the vine. There was nothing else in my stomach. I opened my eyes and the lake had gone. Marcos smiled at me.

"Take a deep breath," he said.

I asked: "How did you get here? Did they let you in?"

"Did you forget? One of them is my mum," he said, taking my hand. "Let's go for a walk. Walking's a good idea."

K

DID YOU MISS THE PLANE? Where are you?

I loved the way Carla talked with her hands, putting her palms together as if to pray, or circling them away, a graceful, dancerly habit, drawing arabesques, airborne spirals, quotation marks, or underlining a point with her slim fingers set off by rings with bright gemstones, the nails painted navy blue, a yellow raffia strip of our Lord of Bonfim, quite threadbare, still tied to her wrist. It was almost hypnotic. Her gestures called my attention to the photos of Rita lying dead at the foot of her staircase—these were spread over the table alongside the expert reports and the dish of *gnocchi al sugo* that she'd made the day before.

The meeting's started. Denise has asked three times where you are.

"I talked to Denis," Carla said, indicating a section in one of the reports. "Serrano is not cheap. He's also not on the circuit any longer, he retired, but I don't know another investigator to touch him."

I read: "12 cm-long hematoma in the lumbar region, small marks indicating internal hemorrhage in the cervical region, left side. Ecchymoses to the chest area."

She said, "Considering the height of the staircase and Rita's height and weight, according to Serrano's analysis, if she had fallen, the autopsy would have found much more extensive internal and external trauma. Serrano also thought it strange that there were no marked abrasions. And there was no blood on the steps."

"So does he rule out an accident?" I asked.

"Patience! There are more tests to run. For now, all we have is evidence."

Why aren't you answering my calls? Carla had spent the morning with Denis comparing the initial police reports, which supported a verdict of accidental death, against those supplied by Serrano.

"The tests also ruled out cardiac issues," Carla said. "Rita was actually quite an athlete."

Carla was opening a bottle of wine when the doorbell rang. I used the pause while she answered the door to check my phone. Seven missed calls from Bia. As I read her fourth message—*Answer this piece of shit, for fuck's sake*—my phone rang again. It was Bia.

Preparing my final report on the three weeks I'd spent in Cruzeiro do Sul had been a huge task. There had been twenty-eight cases heard, followed by nineteen convictions, eight acquittals, and one sentence annulled due to jury contamination. I included the details of each trial, photos and notes as well as my own analysis, and emailed it all to the office, adding that there were still two cases pending final rulings, which I hoped to continue monitoring: the trials of Txupira and Rita's cases.

While Bia was firing a great raft of questions down the line at me, I saw Paulo come into the room behind Carla.

"Have you read my messages? I don't believe you're actually in Acre," Bia was saying.

Paulo gave me a kiss on the forehead and sat down beside me.

"The task force has ended," Bia said. "Denise wants you back here."

Carla went to the kitchen and came back with a plate and cutlery for Paulo.

"Everything's in my email," I told Bia, and hung up without saying goodbye.

Paulo was observing us curiously, attentively, waiting for us to bring him into our discussion, but Carla went on talking about hematomas and ecchymoses discerned by the new investigator as if he weren't there. Even while we finished lunch, she pointed a fork covered in tomato sauce at the section of the report that described lesions in the thyroid cartilage, and said:

"One theory is that Rita sustained a number of blows to the head, probably from behind, and was then strangled and dragged down the stairs, already dead."

We had coffee on the veranda. Paulo was not happy. He went on meekly sitting there, looking at us, saying nothing. When Carla stopping talking, he asked if we'd read the comments beneath the online announcement of the judge's decision to discharge Txupira's original jury. The piece had been published the day before, next to an interview with Carla, whose photo illustrated the page.

I could see the tension between the two of them. Paulo showed us the piece on his phone, then began to read: "São Paulo bitch." "This one won't shut up till she has a good mouthful of worms." "Nice ass for a barbecue." "What wouldn't I do with that tight pussy?" "Hey Carla, when are we going to fuck?" "I could lick that prosecutor's used toilet roll." "Bet she can suck for Brazil."

"Why should I read this kind of crap?" Carla asked.

Paulo was worried—not unreasonably. I was worried, too. Rita's death put us all on edge. But Carla told me later that she thought Paulo was just looking for a pretext to "shack up properly in my house."

"I'm kind of losing patience with Paulo," she said. "There's a touch of the manic-depressive about his behavior. It's been like this since we met. All of a sudden he'll go crazy about, let's say, carpentry—that's just an example, could be anything—and he'll talk and talk and say he wants to do this because he wants a carpentry workshop, because it'll do really well because he was born to start up a carpentry business, he'll have a hundred ideas about aspects of making and restoring furniture, rustic pieces, 'different' pieces, furniture made from reclaimed wood or god knows what, and then he goes and does a carpentry course online, and we buy a hammer and drill bits and a circular saw and a tape measure and an electric drill and a jigsaw and a spirit level and, in the end, he does some average work on lifeboats at a seaside resort town. And then he's all disillusioned with the amazing world of carpentry. And he comes up with a thousand excuses for not getting his carpentry business together:

because there are already lots of carpentry workshops in the city; because there's no market for the kind of carpentry he wants to do; because Brazil is a shitshow; because the taxes in Brazil are too high; because starting a small business in Brazil is enough to send anyone round the bend. All that is true, but I see red when I find he hasn't even unpacked the effing drill bits. Then there's the depressive phases. He gets down about doing so little at the resort, because he's spending whole days sitting outside in killer temperatures. And then he asks to be laid off. And that gets him thinking: What if I set up a little juice business—exotic juices, but made with the local fruits? *Bacuri* juice, *piquiá* juice, graviola, *condessa*, *ingá* juice, *cajarana*, *apuí*. Low phase over, now he's a whirlwind of juice-making. And with that comes the research. Suddenly there are a thousand-and-one things I *have* to read about the economic potential of the fresh juice market. And then we discover the government is offering credit to people wanting to take the leap—and here I go again, back at the bank. And I'm talking to the bank manager. And now we've bought another online course, 'How to start up your small business.' Then, after the euphoria of the juices, and the juice-making class, comes the juice depression. And then the juice thing dies, too, with nothing at all to show for it. And nothing ever really happens."

"Is it always you who pays for the courses?"

"Well, now he's out of work. But when he is working, it's always something short-term, with a low salary. And he has problems at home, with his dad. I'm losing the will, you know? At his age, to be sleeping on a mattress in his parents' living room. In my time, when your kid hit eighteen, they were a grown-up. These days, you kids"—and she meant me, too—"you really take your time getting started."

While we cleaned up the kitchen, she told me her problem was with ending it.

"Starting new relationships is a challenge for me. But finishing them is my 'big problem.' I just can't do it. I spin it out, I stall and prevaricate, make up excuses, stand them up *again*, and it's awful but, I don't know, I always think the guy should get the point that I'm not in the mood anymore without me having to show them the door, but some people really need a full-stop done in steel and concrete. They just go on calling, asking again and again, can I stay over today? What about tomorrow? Or Saturday? And when it doesn't work, they want to play the big guy, freaking me out, saying I need them to protect me, I need a man in my house . . . I mean, why on earth else was he sitting there reading those vile comments out loud to us?"

"What are you going to do?" I asked.

"I already did it," she replied. Seeing Paulo to the door, she said, she had broken with her usual ways and told him that while Rita's case remained unsolved, and in view of its association with Txupira's case, she would have neither the time nor the headspace for anything else.

You really are very self-centered, I told myself, realizing that I was already reassigning the list of faults Carla had outlined, hers and Paulo's, into my own self-flagellations: I was still living with my grandmother & I couldn't bring myself to end relationships & I couldn't really trust people & I was stuck in a rut & I had no idea why I was still in Acre & I couldn't even call the office and tell them I wanted to quit.

That afternoon, instead of calling Bia or Denise, I drove Carla back to the courthouse, put on a bikini, and went swimming in the creek near my house. I swam, then stretched out in the sun and stayed there, staring at the sky; there was nothing else I could do. It was as if my heart and arteries were going into hibernation. My breathing decelerated. Suddenly inside me I could hear Zapira's voice, *anô gueda iu ra rauê gueda*, and I saw the indigenous women's bare feet on the beaten earth, their feet in trainers, in flip-flops, in old football boots, plastic sandals, worn-out old shoes, my own feet, all of us stamping out the beat, *terô, terô, terô, auê*, Zapira's hands weaving *babaçu* palm slings, the wind in the coconut palms and the Lady of the Green Stones, my path through the forest, the giant jatobá nearly one hundred feet tall and little me standing beside that colossal tree (I looked like a doll in the photo Marcos took), our moonlit river swim and the key symbol on my jade stone and the wild-haired warrior women, my thoughts were like wild monkeys, leaping from branch to branch, from the huts of the indigenous village and back to my desk, overflowing with murderers, rapists, harassers, abusers, from the scents of the forest to Amir slapping my face to the jungle growing freely everywhere I looked, and the parrots, the inhambus, the toucans, harpy eagles, trumpeter birds, and the taste of the *cipó* vine in its ayahuasca brew, my feet in the freezing water, and all the traffic of São Paulo, all those cars stuck at crossroads, all those hours and minutes and the air conditioner always on, so much time written off, waiting for the lights to change, for the queue to move, all those buildings on Avenida Paulista where I worked and all that tarmac and all that fear ravaging the city seemed to blend with my fury, a fury rooted deep down, right at the bottom, and the deeper I swam into this fury, the wilder my savage thoughts, leaping onto fresh branches, skipping from my father to how the city consumed our time to the hearings, the never-ending cases—now this appeal and another appeal and yet another appeal—and here I am, right here, with that lovely soft rush of water in my ears and Zapira's rattled rhythm inside me, tint of the urucum, taste of the cipó brew, the hot sun, my body floating in the current, a whole, wholly alive world surrounding me on every side.

I went by the supermarket before heading home. And despite my arms laden with shopping bags, I stopped at the ice cream shop, bought a graviola ice cream, and ate it sitting in the main square, taking my time.

"Ruan . . ." a young mother called her child, who was rooting beneath a rubbish bin and had just recovered an old umbrella nearly twice his height. The boy hefted it in his thin arms as if it were a gun, the kind the dealers use, powerful enough to blow off arms and legs. He scrambled up a couple of steps, soother still in his mouth, leaped over a puddle, and trundled unsteadily toward me.

I couldn't help but laugh when he attacked:

"Hands up! Pow-pow!" he said.

His mother swept him up, threw the umbrella into the bin, and I went home.

As I was parking, I saw there was someone on my veranda.

Only once I'd stepped out of the car could I see him clearly: Amir was sitting on the steps, a beer in one hand, phone in the other. Beside him was a not-insubstantial suitcase.

"Hi," he said, and smiled.

8

KILLED BY HER HUSBAND

Lilian Maria de Oliveira wanted
to turn the volume on the TV up
or down, we cannot be sure which it was.
Her husband,
Cleuber Elias Silva Santos,
wanted the opposite,
the volume lower, should she have asked to raise it,
or higher, should she have wanted less.
Perhaps because they were like this about everything in life,
oil and water, chalk and cheese.
What's for sure is that they fought over who had
the remote control.
I wager: the wife won.
Her husband went to the kitchen, picked up a knife, and
killed her
with one sure stab to the stomach.
"You've killed my Mommy," Lilian's son
said,
hearing his mother
take her last breath.

L

CRUZEIRO DO SUL. My house. *Ding-dong*. Amir opens the door wearing the same psychotic smile with which he welcomed me from the veranda a few hours earlier. He has jettisoned the beer and the suitcase. A young medic with the air of a recent graduate steps inside along with an ambulance driver. I am on the sofa, in a dead faint. Or, more accurately: dead. Noting the post-mortem rigor of my jaw and throat, the medic says, "There is nothing I can do for her."

Since the doctor believes I have killed myself, the morgue arranges to have me taken away. The whole thing is wrapped up very quickly compared to the case of Indizete, a Black girl stabbed by her boyfriend, who had to wait outside on the cold asphalt, beside her fallen saucepan and the feijão stew mixed with her blood, ten, twelve, eventually eighteen hours before, like me, being weighed and washed with soap and water in the autopsy room.

They cut me open from neck to pubis and examine my insides. They hunt for lesions, wounds, poison-damaged tissues. They peel away my scalp from ear to ear and take out my brain. They use a power saw to cut through the casing of my skull. Sadly, my thoughts aren't there, or they'd be undergoing the same painstaking analysis as my heart and my guts.

The report indicates suicide by ingestion of a potent combination of sleeping pills, alcohol, and a dash of rat poison. A note, found beside my bed by Amir, corroborates the verdict of self-destruction:

Amir, take my body to São Paulo. I want to be cremated there and for my ashes to be scattered on the beach at Cabritas, where we spent New Year's. Our love is forever. Look after Grandma. None of this is your fault.

Later, my note is added to the legal proceedings by Amir, who describes how he came to Cruzeiro do Sul after noticing that his girlfriend, by whom he meant intrepid little me, was depressed.

The slow-moving legal machine creaks into action. They do more tests on my blood and my belly region. Handwriting tests. The prosecution uses these to demonstrate that the suicide note was written by Amir. I was murdered. But the defense hires cowboy investigators and proves that the letters *d* from *depressed*, *s* from *suicide*, *m* from *morbid*, *o* from *orphan*, and *f* from *fucked* contain features peculiar to my handwriting.

Because I am white, middle-class, and pretty to boot, the press won't leave us alone. I am never out of the newspapers. I'm their fallen star. Without permission, they recycle photos I posted online—me on the beach and in the countryside, me with elephants in Kenya, me on the Eiffel Tower, me in a boat, with friends, running, eating ice cream, me with Amir, me doing yoga—to illustrate the bittersweet (ideal of purity and youth) and life's idiotic unfairness (the obverse of life = murdered maiden).

Defendant Amir is also our hero. His face is so ubiquitous and his ascent to fame so vertiginous that many young boys and teens start to consider killing their girlfriends so they too can have the abs they see on defendant Amir in the fast-moving online press.

All of this means that the judicial system begins to tick over at a fair lick—*ma non troppo*.

At the trial, which would only have been held in seven, eight, maybe ten years' time if I'd been Black, or wouldn't have been held at all if I were poor, the defense will say there was no kinder person on this Earth, no one more upright, more ethical, more humane than Defender of the Realm (ha) Amir. Defendant Amir and dead princess-me make a gorgeous couple.

In accordance with the law, Amir is not borderline anything, nor a proper psychopath—not even *Homo constantissimus*. Amir is *Homo medius*. He gets jealous. He can't tolerate betrayal or disobedience. Nothing sticks to him. He is an exemplary professional, a well-behaved citizen, and a voter for the incumbent president. Round of applause!

And I, in the eyes of the law—I am Eve. Gentlemen, she ate the apple, the defense will claim. To get the lowdown on me, you've only to cast your eye over the *Malleus Maleficarum*. Here I am, on defendant Amir's left—naked. I have demonic intentions. I sleep with Satan. Gentlemen, this girl prepared potions with goats' hooves and snakes' eyes. You know what this is?

They tear me apart during the hearing. What were my red nails for, anyway? Scratching, of course. And my mouth? To suck his dick. And my breasts? For nursing. And my tongue? For cursing and tattling. And my hands? For washing, cooking, and ironing. For chopping, grinding, kneading, and throwing out. And my genitals? For procreating and for straying. And my bottom? For looking good on city billboards.

My thoughts whirled round and round as I waited for Amir to reach the restaurant.

I had refused to talk to him on my veranda. As soon as I saw him, I got straight back in the car, terrified. I had read too many cases of women murdered by their husbands, boyfriends, brothers, fathers, ex-boyfriends, or lovers simply to say, "Hi, Amir, let's go in and get a coffee while I officially terminate our relationship."

In our homes is where we're dying. They kill us over our farewells.

"Meet me at Pomar's," I called, from the car.

I just barely heard his answer: "I don't have a car!"

Let him go on foot. Let him crawl. Or take a taxi. I was not about to let a man who'd slapped me get into my car.

"See what you've done?" I said to my grandmother on the phone while I waited for Amir. "Now he's washed up here."

"He's a good boy. He's desperate to get back together with you . . . "

"He is not a good boy. I don't want you to speak to him anymore. No more, okay?"

"Coming to Acre," she said, "proves that he loves you."

"He slapped me in the face," I shouted, feeling the statement in my body. All the blood seemed to have gathered in my face while my heart beat down in my belly.

I could almost hear my grandma crumbling on the other end.

"He did that?" she asked.

"Yes," I replied.

A long silence.

"He hit you?"

"Yes."

"Is that why you left?"

"That's why."

"When?"

"At Bia's party."

"And what else?"

"Should there be anything else?"

"Are you hiding something from me? I want to know exactly what happened."

"He slapped me. And called me a whore."

"Why?"

"Why what? You want to know if I deserved it?"

"Don't speak to me like that. Not to me!" she shouted.

A long silence.

"Did he rape you?"

"No."

"Amir raped you and you won't tell me."

"He slapped me. The way I see it, a slap in the face is a moral rape."

"I want to know everything he did."

"He's coming," I said. "I have to hang up."

My grandma started shouting on the other end.

"Don't talk to him. Don't let him come close. Get out of there right away."

I hung up.

"Hi Amir," I said.

He stood his suitcase next to the table and sat down. My telephone began to ring.

"I've come here feeling like the lowest kind of man," he said. "You're afraid of me. Even worse: I gave you reason to be afraid."

The waiter came to take our order.

"Would you like a juice?" I asked.

"Anything," he replied.

I ordered passion fruit juices for both of us. When the waiter had gone, Amir stated, with some solemnity, that he would never, ever, ever ever ever again lay a finger on me. Ever.

"Do you believe me?"

"I believe you," I lied.

I had decided not to argue. Not to provoke or disagree or play anything down. Not to fan flames or take bait. All I wanted was to end it.

He said: "I'd dropped an acid tab at the party. I was totally out of my head. You never gave me a chance to explain."

"I understand."

"Do you forgive me?" he asked.

"Of course. Acid lets out the beast inside us," I said.

Grandma was still trying to talk to me. I turned off my phone.

Amir laid his hands over mine.

"If I'd known what happened to your mother . . . " he said.

" . . . you would never have slapped me in the face," I finished for him.

I don't know how that flew out of my mouth. I didn't want to fight. I'd thought of copying the female dragonflies' strategy to fend off males wanting sex: they drop out of the air and lie still on the ground, playing dead.

"I was going to say something else," he said.

"I know what you were going to say. You'd have said, 'Gosh, it must be a real pain that your dad killed your mum, and then, on top of that, to have me knocking you around, too. A hassle, really.' You'll have been thinking the women in my family are quite messed up, one already pushing up daisies, now this one taking her turn being slapped around—that really is a lot of marital terror for one small family."

I silently called myself to order. If Amir was like a hippo, I thought, smearing his shit around in his attempts to captivate a female, I could only be a dragonfly playing dead. Don't be an idiot, I told myself. No call for suicide here. Not a word more. Say the problem is you, be a dragonfly faker, say you have commitment problems, blame your murdered mum, blame your overbearing grandma, let him feel like the triumphant male, let him feel sorry for you, and get the hell out of this place.

The waiter brought our juices.

"I'm the problem," I said, trying to get back on track. (And with major regret that I hadn't caught Amir's expression just then on camera.)

"It's me," I said again. "I can't commit to a man who's slapped me in the face. It's a problem I have, a professional hazard. I prefer unaggressive men, gentle men. It's a personality glitch, I know. But for me, a man who'll hit a woman is only warming up to what he really wants to do, which is killing women. I don't know why but I can't sleep with a potential murderer."

Amir gave a long sigh. Two patches of sweat began to widen across his shirt.

"Listen, Amir," I said. "I know you're feeling bad. I feel awful, too."

His phone began to ring. He picked it up and showed me the screen with Grandma's name flashing on it.

"My adviser," he said, proudly, hoping to appease me. "Hi, Dona Yolanda," he spoke into the phone. "Guess who's here with me?"

That was all he managed. Even from where I was sitting, I could hear the noise of Grandma's fury down the line. Amir sat in front of me, telephone stuck to his ear, listening and turning white, listening and listening, something like a car in a disassembly line, losing its wheels, steering, axles . . . I've no idea what Grandma said. When he hung up, the man before me was a pale shadow of the Amir I'd known.

We finished our juices in silence.

"I'll try to get a flight back to Rio Branco today," he said.

I shrugged. I took one more sip of juice, this time slurping loudly through my straw. He used to hate me doing that when we were going out.

"If I have to stay until tomorrow, which hotels would you recommend?"

"The Eldorado," I said. "Or the Excelsior."

"I'll never forgive myself," he said, getting up. He pulled out his wallet but I wouldn't let him pay.

"You're my guest today," I said. More slurping.

At the door, he tried to kiss my cheek but I stuck out my hand, a spear aimed at him.

I called Grandma from the car.

"What did you say to him?" I asked.

"That I know now about him slapping you. That if he didn't make himself scarce, if he didn't keep well away from you and me, I would show up at his office and kick up a scandal on a scale he's never seen. And if this didn't work, I would hire a professional assassin to finish him off. And that, after blowing his brains out, my hitman would be sent to sort out his sister, his father, and his mother, there'd be no one left in his family to perpetuate the name. He will never forget that phone call, my darling."

I giggled, euphoric. We laughed together for a good while. I asked her three times to tell me the whole story again, and each time we laughed some more. Word for word, I begged, I want you to tell it like that again, and she went over it once more, and again, and then I felt oddly moved, like the night of the full moon when the warriors of the Green Stones and I went out with our bows and arrows to hunt for Crisântemo, my excitement at stuffing the rapist into the trunk of my car and the satisfaction of driving him into the jungle, where we'd kicked his face until he hadn't a tooth left in it, hahahahaha, and we'd burst his eyes with our spears, hahahahaha, and cut off that predator's dick, hahahahahahahahahaha, the same dick he had forced on Txupira's pussy before hanging her from a butcher's hook, my joy at lopping off his legs and arms, we chopped him up completely, put his pieces in a pan, cooked it all till he was cooked right through and then we fed him to our wild dogs, our wolves and fierce leopards, our insatiable jaguars.

"Don't stay home by yourself tonight," my grandmother instructed, before we hung up.

I followed her advice. I went to Marcos's place and stayed there for the rest of the week.

DELTA

Ob-la-di ob-la-da life goes on bra / La-la how their life goes on.
    The ritual is always the same. Everything takes place around the lake, in the very center of the forest where we warriors come together, although this time with longer arrows embellished with swallow feathers, long enough to cross oceans. We bathe, receive our green stone of the day, and then follow the ritual with one small variation. This time, instead of singing *terô, terô, auê, anô gueda iu ra rauê queda*, I teach everyone to sing *Ob-la-di ob-la-da*, and unthinkingly, I start to sing it myself the moment my eyes fall on the mysterious key sign engraved in my green stone, a cue that jolts me back to a vision: a knot of keys swinging in the ignition of a car I don't recognize, the keys are glinting and jingling, I am afraid and I am little, sitting in the back seat, and I can see the dashboard of this car I don't know, it has a strange smell, and the radio is playing and the tune I'm hearing is *Ob-la-di ob-la-da life goes on bra*, and then my vision fades like smoke and the warrior women are singing with me, *Ob-la-di ob-la-da life goes on bra . . .* They don't want to know the rest of the lyrics, they don't care about Desmond and Molly Jones's story, they just like *Ob-la-di ob-la-da*. For them, Desmond is only a husband and husbands, boyfriends, brothers, fathers, grandfathers, uncles, cousins,

neighbors, every one of these men is an enemy, and why bother with enemies if we're finally living in a land without men? Besides which, Desmond—it seems highly likely—no longer really tolerates Molly singing with her own band in the evenings. Instead of giving Molly a twenty-carat golden ring, he pushes her around, kicks and rapes her, and Molly's pretty face now displays one black eye and a cut lip, and the home they built together becomes a slaughterhouse for Molly. Hence the warrior women don't care to hear Desmond's story. *Ob-la-di ob-la-da*, they sing loudly, wildly, with maximum enthusiasm, and the one yelling it the loudest is Txupira.

This Txupira is in a very different state from the girl who appeared in the police reports; she is unwounded, without lesions, without glass in her uterus and with ribs unbroken, eyes unpunctured, unmutilated, she is whole and healthy, except that she no longer has her genitals. Here they've stuck the same black strip that the censors, in certain periods, would stick over redacted text.

"Where's Txupira's vagina?" I ask, and the women tell me that her vagina is free now, winged like a bird, and its mission is to pursue and terrorize her murderers.

"It's what we usually do with non-consensual sex cases," they explain. They're really enjoying this story. How they laugh. Giggling, one of them says that during the attacks, the glands of flying clitorises grow rigid and turn into points as hard and resistant as drill bits—"a deadlier kind of *vagina dentata*," she says. "Imagine all those abusers, those grabbers, those sexual terrorists, sitting in a classroom, for example, when suddenly, *whoosh*, they get a cunting to the head, puncturing their brains with the efficiency of an electric drill. But first Txupira's vagina hovers over them and pisses on their heads."

"Our flying vaginas are as powerful as anacondas," says another. "They can swallow a rapist whole, *schloop*, in a single gulp, then regurgitate him straight into the land of the dead."

"Wait and see what we'll do with that man who likes to grab women by the pussy."

All the warriors, Txupira, too, are weak from laughter, they're bent double with it, beating their feet and hands on the ground as they picture all the terrified machos trying to escape our airborne vaginas.

So it goes: half our meeting is pure amusement. The other half is hard work.

Now that we've laughed and sung and swum, our Lady of the Green Stones asks, "What shall we tackle today, girls?"

I have everything prepared, so I speak up:

"Here are the photos of Abelardo Ribeiro Maciel and Antônio Francisco Medeiros, who, in my opinion, should meet the same fate as Crisântemo. After all, they both helped Crisântemo to kill Txupira."

Txupira likes the idea. Txupira would like to break every bone in their two bodies, not forgetting the smallest fingerbone but starting with their spines, arms, and legs, then crushing their hands, feet, and toes with our *cupania*-wood staffs. Txupira wants to perforate their lungs, and for this reason carries everywhere a sheaf of arrows with razor-sharp *taquara* tips. She wants to tear out their hearts with her hands. She describes all this while cleaning her nails, which still have dried blood under them.

"How long are we going to keep killing rich white men?" asks the tallest warrior.

Another says, yawning, "I also have a major list of men I'd like to kill."

I say again that Antônio Francisco Medeiros and Abelardo Ribeiro Maciel must die. I'm not sure why but the warriors seem to be looking to me for some leadership. They discuss with their eyes still on me.

"Now," says our Lady of the Green Stones, "our hatred is multipurpose. There are many ways we could channel it. There is no obligation to wage war against men forever."

"There is a fundamental difference between unihatred and multipurpose hatred," another woman explains. "A civilizing difference."

"That's why the men were expelled from this land," says the Lady of the Green Stones.

"What are we talking about?" I ask. "Are we going to roll over and be nice little women now?"

"She needs to understand," says another.

"She" is me, that much is clear.

The Lady of the Green Stones goes on: "We all know that men have a tendency to be aggressive—we all have that tendency, but men, well—imagine a reservoir of aggression. Every time men hear a 'no,' every time someone, generally a woman, disobeys them, every time they get into an argument in traffic, every time they lose an election or lose their status or lose a bet, a game, some money, every time they get drunk, every time they're reprimanded, every time a plan falls through, every time they can't get it up or we laugh at them or reject them, the reservoir fills a little more. Then, when they get one more tongue-lashing from their boss, or their team loses the championship yet again, their currency crashes, the car in front cuts them off, their mate gets a raise, the sensation of being opposed becomes more fuel on their fire and their reservoir of aggression rises higher and higher, filling with repressed aggression, and this aggression must be released on a regular basis so it doesn't explode the reservoir or even kill its bearer by giving him a heart attack. And then it is released. The gates open. All that lavaggression floods out onto—who? Women. Killing women is the safety valve of choice for would-be Alpha males' unihatred. Of course this is only generally speaking. One flank of our would-be Alphas targets immigrants, Black and/or poor people, gay and trans people, but the majority, the great majority, focuses the whole of their hatred on women. Our would-be Alphas are univiolent. This is why they were banished from our paradise. So our hatred can do many things. We are here to discuss: What should we be doing with our hatred?"

"Hold on there," I say. "Where I'm from, women are doing whatever the hell they want. We set new records every day. We're running major institutions, time-tabling out our futures, forging global strategies. We're also dying like mosquitoes, we earn less than men, we play our part in politics, we file complaints at the police station, we run marathons, we go on horrendous diets— inhuman diets—we operate machines, we get divorced, we eat badly, we draw up diagrams as intricate as Beethoven's symphonies, we go for low-grade jobs, we hose down the underworld, we spread ourselves too thin, we are squalid, we chop and broil, we die of fright, we make deals with our enemies, we betray each other, we have our fingers in hundreds of pies, we clean toilets, we get murdered, we get hungry, we take lovers, we weep in our mother's laps, we are walked out on, we are slaves in our own homes, we cheat, we divorce, we remarry, we live in fear, we tell our tragedies to the police (who laugh in our faces), and we mastermind massive scams. Huge operations. We women, highly specialized, deeply exploited, deeply domestic, one hundred percent stressed. We work eighteen hours a day. Eighteen hours is our working day—eighteen hours of fear and hard work, at home and everywhere else. Cleaning up filth, organizing, fighting back, planning, being beaten, tidying drawers, getting pregnant, driving, ironing and washing. We are efficient. This leaves men with a dilemma: it's a question of time.

We are on the way to occupying every position. We'll soon be booting them off the driving seat; they can try being passengers."

"We already tried that," one woman says.

And the chorus responds.

"That won't work."

"They're violent."

"We do have one major advantage," I say. "Our vaginas."

They laugh.

"You're all lower down the pecking order."

"You should banish them."

"We're very parsimonious with them. They're only used for procreation these days."

"Many species work like this. Some females kill their males after copulation. We're really such good girls, considering."

"That isn't the issue today," says our Lady of the Green Stones. "To return to my initial question: What shall we do now?"

I say, "We have priorities."

"We can all choose," another suggests. "There are women here who use their hatred to peel cassavas."

I say, "Please: you can peel cassava when I'm gone. I came to you for something else. We have an unfinished mission—and I say again that Abelardo Ribeiro Maciel and Antônio Francisco Medeiros must die. They complete the trio."

"Death to them both," Txupira shouts.

And Txupira's commitment carries the day.

"What's the plan?" asks the Lady of the Green Stones.

I open a canvas toolbag that I've brought with me. Inside are guns as black as a *graúna*'s wings.

They put down their bows and arrows and, intrigued, they come over, one by one, to pick through my guns. One of them is still humming softly under her breath: *Ob-la-di ob-la-da . . .*

"We'll learn to use them in a moment," I say, "but first of all, take a look at this." I pull a map from my bag and lay it out on the grass. The warrior women gather around. I describe my plan.

M

MARCOS HAD A PLAN.

"If you want to understand the overall concept," he said, "you have to believe in Cruzeiro do Sul as a mystical preserve, a privileged space where the final stage of evolution will take place, the last act of a spiritual revolution, which began way back with the Egyptians and that lot, which travelled via the Holy Land, following the path of our rotation around the sun, from East to West, and which, as we know, ends here, right at our feet."

For Marcos, it was no accident that the city was full of Masonic lodges, spiritual centers, and candomblé assemblies.

"You don't find anyone round here pulling down Umbanda meeting houses or fighting over faith issues the way they do in other Brazilian towns," he said. "Actually, our awareness of our spiritual significance is what underpins the brotherly ecumenism here in Cruzeiro."

Nor was it "mere coincidence" that precisely here on our planet a powerful shamanic tradition based around the ingestion of ayahuasca, "which lets us speak directly to God and to our dead," was still alive and kicking.

"One of the most important tasks of the new world order will be dealing with the trauma of the animals now suffering from human cruelty," Marcos went on. "You can't imagine how bummed the whole animal world is with us right now. And I don't just mean the bulls and cows and chickens, which live and die in the cruelest ways. I mean, the bees are livid, the whales—shit, you can't get your head around how much the whales can't stand us, they've had to eat so many tons of plastic bags; the leopards are depressed, the monkeys and frogs the same; there's hardly a species out there that doesn't hate us deeply for having pursued an animal massacre unequaled in the history of the world. If you're thinking about ends being nigh, we're more effective than wildfires, floods, hurricanes, or earthquakes. There is nothing to match human potential when it comes to finishing off the animal world."

Marcos's plan was to create a rehabilitation center for traumatized animals, using cipó vine tea as the basis for treatment. He had already done experiments on his own dog, Tadeu, who had been badly beaten by his previous owner, which Marcos believed had led to the dog's habit of eating shit.

"See how smart animals are," he said. "Tadeu started eating horse, ox, and goat droppings so he would get sick, because he knew he wouldn't be beaten if he was sick."

I asked if he'd ever met his dog's last owner.

"You should be asking a different question," he said. "How do I know my dog used to eat feces? You might think I'm just another loony ayahuasca disciple, but even so I'll tell you: I converse with my dog. And I don't mean I'm like one of those old bachelors who think they're talking to their cats and it's genuine interspecies dialogue. My chats with Tadeu are different. The 'huasca puts us in a mental space where we share a universal language. We don't use words. We have an experiential exchange. I offer him my love, my happiness, my sadness, and Tadeu does the same—but on an informational level. It was Tadeu who helped me realize how massively traumatized our whole animal world has become due to human behavior. All we've done, over the last few centuries, was abuse and destroy whole species."

Every time we visited the Ch'aska community, Marcos would talk to Zapira about his project of creating this model veterinary clinic which would be part of the imminent new order. Zapira listened to him in silence, savoring her snuff or smoking her herb cigarette, thoughtful and disbelieving, unsure whether or not to let Marcos have the ayahuasca vine for his experiments—which had to date been done using the doses that his mother, Zapira's cousin, had secretly put aside in plastic bottles and smuggled to her son, always asking him to be discreet.

I told Carla about all this on her birthday, while we ate ice cream at her house. She seemed strangely sad. When I arrived with flowers, wine, and the ice cream, I'd been surprised to find I was the only guest for dinner, which, being so wiped out, she had not in fact prepared. We'd dined on ice cream, on the veranda, as she recounted her tough week in court, defending women charged with what the law calls minor infractions: slander, minor body wounds, mistreatment, breaking and entering.

"The thing is never-ending. It's like trying to mop the floor with the tap on full. Exit one poor woman, here comes another.

My work is basically dealing with an endless line of screwed-up women," she said. "They come and talk to me in the breaks between hearings. They're so full of guilt. Lots of them still love the men they're trying to send down. They want to drop charges, they want to stop the case, but the law won't let them. 'We've already sorted things out between him and me,' they tell me. 'Can't we close the case?' I explain that we can't and they fly off the handle. If the guy's already behind bars, they suffer because their kids don't have a dad. They suffer because they're vulnerable, because they want to keep their family together, because they have no money. They don't even have the cash to go see their man in prison. And if they do have it, they suffer in long lines, hours and hours in the sun, in the rain, and then they're humiliated by the officers doing strip searches. Today I managed to get the sentence of an asshole who disfigured his girlfriend commuted from prison with immediate effect to preventive detention. I thought the girl would be happy but she practically assaulted me. 'I didn't want him to get arrested,' she said. I asked: 'What did you want?' 'For him to stop beating me,' she replied. 'That's all.'"

"She doesn't realize she'll be back on the kitchen floor in no time," I said.

"But prison doesn't solve the problem either," Carla said. "The truth is, while our best legal avenue for protecting women from this kind of violence does mark a major achievement for the victims, on the other hand, it also creates a raft of problems for them. We've dumped everything in the same box: homicide along with slander, domestic quarrels, and attempted homicide.

There's no way it can work. Seriously, sometimes I wonder what we're doing here. This is no place for the state. It's a penal system turned upside down. We incarcerate at the drop of a hat and in so doing, we create a heap of problems for the prisoner's family—and for the state. Because all our carceral system gives the guy who's in prison for hitting his woman is criminal savvy and an even shorter fuse. I'm not saying the Maria da Penha domestic violence law is no good. But it's not the solution. These days we might not even give pretrial detention to an aggressor, so the guy goes free, and less than twenty-four hours later, we learn the next thing he did was strangle and chop-suey the woman who took him to court."

Carla was also upset because she was losing her only assistant.

"When I got here," she said, "I had two assistants. Six months later, the state took one away from me. Now I haven't even got one. There used to be three judges; now there's only one. There were three defending counsels; now just the one. The state is taking it all away. You can't even make a coffee in the courthouse anymore. And the work only increases. Sometimes we hear twenty cases in a single day—twenty! Other counties only see that many in a week."

That afternoon she had taken one of the breaks to go and discuss Txupira's case with the judge and had found him lying on a sofa.

"'Too tired to talk,' he'd said. I thought about the two of us there, and well, shit, we're well and truly fucked. In this heat," Carla went on, "we're forced to stay inside in full air-conditioning, and it's like being in a freezer. The people are dying of cold, they say. So we turn the air-con off. Then, when we can't stand the fug anymore, we turn the air-con back on. And when we finally get out of there, the corridors have become ovens, same with the streets. And a few minutes later, we're back in the freezer. Freezer-oven-freezer-oven. Then, when the AC finally breaks down, we're practically cooked during the hearings."

After all that, telling Carla about Marcos's plans let a bit of light into our conversation. Her rich, ringing laugh soon had me giggling, too.

"So his dog talks back to him now?" she wanted to know.

"He says it does."

"What does it say?"

"It was the dog itself that said it used to eat shit."

She was crying with laughter.

I said: "He's a sure-fire golden goose, you'll see."

"Is he good in bed?" she asked.

"We get on well. I like him."

"He's not too much of an overgrown boy for you?"

But before I could answer, she said, "Look who's talking. Paulo is twelve years younger than me. Must be some kind of occupational hazard for us, don't you think? We see so many shit men in court, so many turds, that we lose our taste for a certain kind of man completely. The 'full-grown' kind. We start thinking that a twenty-year-old kid hasn't yet had time to turn into a total crook. We think we can shape them ourselves."

Less than an hour later, both of us had drunk too much wine and were beached in front of a horrendous TV show, the kind that confines random people in a house together and leaves them to fight in there for an undefined period, eliminating each other and winning prizes. This felt very depressing for a birthday party.

"Let's go dancing," I said. "Let's go out."

While I waited for Carla to get ready, I received a message from Bia. *Just to let you know, they're dismissing you. With just cause: abandonment of post. I didn't even dare try to defend you. Where on earth have you got to?*

When I turned off my phone, Carla was standing there in a red dress with red lipstick and red sandals. She looked quite the she-devil.

"What's up?" she asked.

"They gave me the sack."

"Really? I only just got ready. Can we celebrate?"

We went to the city's most popular nightclub. But first Carla made me put on a black mini-dress of hers. "Everyone will see my ass in this!" I complained, in front of the mirror.

It had been a while since I'd drunk this much. In the club, we stood on the balcony just inside the door and each sank two shots of whisky. Wild.

Then we slipped out to the middle of the dance floor. The music was what you might call "epileptic," the lights, too. The kind of setup that makes you dance like you're channeling Satan. We only stopped to drink more shots of whatever: vodka, rum, and another whisky. Then more frenetic dancing. It was a night of catharsis. We were flushing out all the shit we'd seen in court; Amir, too; each of us had our personal fallout to shed here.

Then Carla yanked my face around to hers.

"I'm going to throw up in the ladies', back soon."

I stayed there, dancing with my eyes closed. Now and then I'd bump into someone; I got elbowed away a few times. I should throw up too, I thought. But suddenly I felt something holding me still and, when I opened my eyes, Crisântemo, Abelardo, and Antônio were dancing around me. Dancing is the wrong word. Crisântemo pressed his body up close.

"So you're the prosecutor's latest bit on the side?" he slurred in my ear.

I gave him a shove, but Abelardo held me back.

"If you're into sucking pussy, gotta be 'cause you haven't learned to suck cock."

I felt the blood leave my face. My drunkenness was, simply, over. Then Paulo appeared from god knows where and dragged me out of there.

"They were threatening me," I said, as he sat me down at the bar. My legs were shaking.

Carla turned up a few minutes later. Paulo told her what had happened. Enraged, drunk, and shoeless, Carla wanted to have a word with them.

"Those shits think they'll intimidate me," she said. "Now's my time to push through a prison sentence for all three."

"Don't," Paulo said, trying to reason with her. "What they want is precisely for you to lose your head."

He took us both outside.

"Where's the car?" he asked.

I managed to find the key in my bag but neither Carla nor I could remember where we'd parked.

With immense patience, Paulo managed to find the vehicle and maneuver us both into it.

"You're in no condition to drive," he said. "I'll take you back."

I wanted to leave Carla at her place and go home but Carla was categorical.

"No way you're going home by yourself. Let's stay at my house. Don't argue!"

After she'd sent Paulo home, I learned the real reason.

"I didn't want him staying here," she said, and fixed up the living room sofa.

"You sleep in my room. It's more comfortable." But when she went to the bathroom, I sank onto the sofa and was asleep in seconds.

9

KILLED BY HER HUSBAND
WITH ASSISTANCE FROM THE STATE

A telephone recording:
Woman: I want . . . just, there's a fight going on here, I don't
know if they're a couple, the woman is shouting for help here
in the street . . .
Policeman: Complaint registered, Senhora. A police car will be
right there, all right?
Woman: Right. Thank you.
Policeman: Of course.

Another recording, same case:
Man: My neighbor here is beating his wife, and there's a kid
with them, I think he's hitting the kid too . . .
Policeman: What's the street name?
Man: São Simeão.
Policeman: São Simeão? There's already a case open for this
location, okay?
Man: Okay.

Yet another recording, same case:
Policeman: Is there an emergency?
Woman: Yes, it's a real emergency, we already called about three times, the guy is killing his wife here and no one's come yet.
Policeman: The incident has already been registered with us (...) The local squad, they're handling the incident right now, you'll just have to wait ...
Woman: We're going to end up falling asleep just waiting for no one to come from the police ...
Policeman: You'll have to wait, Senhora, the incident has been registered.
Woman: Okay.

New recording, same case:
Policeman: Good evening, what is the emergency?
Man: My stepson is here in my house, he says he's killed his wife over on Rua São Simeão.
Policeman: He said he's killed his wife?
Man: That's right, he's covered in blood. I've called her family and they're going over to see ...

Eight neighbors had called the Military Police that night.
But when the police arrived,
almost four hours after the start of the attack,
Daniela Eduarda Alves, thirty-four,
had been dead for twenty minutes.

N

THE SUN FELT LIKE A WEIGHT to be borne on your head. *Zep, zip, ksta, zak* . . . there was a brusque ring to the Kuratawa's language, like a machete scything through the jungle. The children, who had been playing with the shell of a dead jabuti tortoise out in the empty waste ground, now gathered around us, noisy with laughter and chattering things we couldn't understand. Carla, Marcos, and I had just got out of the car. Txupira's sister Janina had seen us and right away left the group, to reappear moments later with her mother and two other indigenous women beside her, women I recognized from the hearing.

Like the indigenous people of the Ch'aska village, the Kuratawa don't go around naked. Brightly colored surf shorts, T-shirts, faded football shirts, old jeans, tattered cotton things, caps, flip-flops, or battered trainers made up their wardrobes. On their home turf and without the urucum designs that had so scandalized the chamber at Txupira's hearing, the women seemed harder to class as indigenous than they did in the urban setting where I'd first met them. One of them, the youngest, with a child on her hip, explained in passable Portuguese that the men of the village had gone out to hunt curassow birds. I later found out that the children had been learning to read and write their native language at the local school—although it had been shuttered since the new government came into power—so they didn't learn Portuguese until the age of nine. Only the men, who travelled more regularly into the city, could really speak Brazil's official language.

Carla hadn't meant for us to spend the whole of Saturday afternoon here, but Marcos decided that, even if the hunters returned late in the evening, waiting for them would be better than having to come back another day, especially as the roads were in a very poor state already, thanks to the rain. The journey had taken five hours when it ought to have been done in three. Carla agreed. It was important to let Txupira's family know how her case was progressing.

We were escorted inside one of the huts stacked together in a chaotic cluster amid young *buriti* and *cepa* palms. All around them, overflowing from an old fuel drum which served as a bin and mingling with the foliage creeping through everywhere, were drifts of soda bottles and plastic wrappings.

In front of the low door covered with babaçu matting, two little boys were playing with old buckets, pans, and dusty mixing bowls, all apparently no longer used in the village.

I was briefly blinded as I stepped inside that dark space, which felt like a planetarium, with its many tiny dots of light studding the roof's dense mesh of babaçu leaves. The first thing I saw was an almost-empty pack of noodles lying beside an oil can. Where many aspects of Zapira's village seemed fresh and charming thanks to the complexity and originality of their craftsmanship, here we met only poverty and deprivation. A powerful smell of frying filled the place. At the back, an older lady was weaving what looked like a colorful hammock.

"How pretty," I said.

Instantly she stood up and left. On the battery-powered radio, a Rihanna track was playing, seemingly to nobody. The old lady soon returned with a hammock in her arms.

"Fitteen real," she said. "Fitteen. Fitteen. Fitteen real."

(Months later, this item would occupy the coziest corner in my grandmother's house.)

The scalding, super-sweet coffee we were offered combined with the sight of so many soda bottles among the litter outside explained why some of the children clustering around us in the compound already had rotten front teeth.

Until now, the only indigenous community I'd visited had been that of the Ch'aska, whose larger and more isolated territories contained plenty of game for their residents. In this Kuratawa community, sliced in two by the BR-364 highway and surrounded by private agricultural land, the situation was quite different. There were none of the great hardwood trees left here, nor any space for indigenous crops, nor even for wild animals. "Capybaras, wild pigs, peccaries, pacas, all of them used to be plentiful but they're rare now," Marcos explained. "You can still see *lambari*, redtail catfish and *manjuba* anchovy in the rivers, but all of them are contaminated with agricultural runoff."

I was not some overexcited tourist demanding a spectacle of folklore, all pendants and plumes. I had been in Cruzeiro do Sul long enough to know the difficulties facing the indigenous communities in the region. But the Kuratawa hardly seemed like an indigenous people; they were simply very poor. And abandoned. I felt heartsick at the sight of it. Increases in the region's population had meant a reduction in the village's own areas for cultivation. Practically no one here was still planting their own cassava or beans. Most of them ate only products they bought in the city's supermarkets with the money they received from the government's "Family Grant." Many of them made a living by selling basic crafts in the city.

All of this, as Marcos would explain later on our way back to Cruzeiro, was part of the long fallout from the disastrous occupation of Acre. The rubber barons had arrived here from the North-East, armed to the teeth and fully intending to enslave the indigenous peoples in service of rubber plantations. Those who rebelled were either killed or forced to flee. Dozens of communities were devastated. "Some people say the indigenous kids were tossed in the air and hooked in the belly on the tips of pikes," he said. "I don't doubt it. Those bush barons whose names are all over the towns around here were butchers. One of them hunted my grandmother down. She was offered as a bonus to some bastard rubber-tapper. Even now these people don't stick to the official demarcation of indigenous lands. They still dream of taking back their land, but now their main aim is agribusiness; they want to burn down the jungle and turn it into grazing."

Tired of waiting, tormented by the heat, we decided to go for a swim in the nearby river. A troupe of children and teenagers followed us.

I felt nervous getting into the same water that was killing the fish.

"If you get to thinking like that, you wouldn't be able to swim anywhere at all," Marcos said. "We're all living in a great soup of agricultural toxins. Take it easy."

There I was, floating along. Marcos and Carla were playing with the kids. A shiver ran through my body every time I remembered Amir's face, dumbstruck, with my grandma's voice in his ear. He'd looked like a climber falling off a precipice. Actually, it had been like watching a play: the drama of an impotent man. The drama of a man whose own arrogance is shoved up his ass; of a man who would never have the last word again. A man who was put in his place. He would not forget that moment, I knew. Beneath that bright blue sky, feeling the sun's heat in my skin, I started to chuckle and swallowed a few gulps of water. When I surfaced again, the young woman who'd spoken some Portuguese before had appeared beside me and was staring at me with a serious expression. Her name was Naia and she was fifteen, a year older than Txupira when she died. We swam together to the far bank.

I asked if she knew the place where Txupira had been seen for the last time.

"Yeh," she said.

"Can we go there?" I asked.

She pointed to a canoe pulled up on the bank.

I asked: "Will you take me?"

Carla didn't want to go: there was nothing around here she hadn't seen already, she said. Marcos would have liked to come, but the kids were using him as a trampoline.

I felt completely out of shape next to this muscled, agile girl who rowed strongly and steadily—especially when I realized she was pregnant.

We advanced slowly toward the forest, watching the Coke-colored water grow darker and muddier. During the journey—which was longer and slower than I'd expected—I noticed marks on Naia's forearms and on her waist, above the buttocks.

"What's that?" I asked.

She didn't reply. But the fact that only the men spoke Portuguese in this community showed clearly where the power lay among the Kuratawa. And then I realized that there had been no complaints filed by indigenous women against their partners in any of the cases I'd seen in Acre. Did they not file complaints? Didn't they have any?

Carla explained later that the women's support services did not reach them. But alcohol did, and that left deep damage.

I inquired once more about Naia's bruises when we were stepping from the canoe into the yellow waters beside a *sapê* plantation. This time I saw she had tried to cover them with her wet T-shirt.

"Was it your husband?" I asked, as she helped me climb the slippery, eroded bank. "He isn't allowed to do that," I said. "No one is," I repeated, emphatically. "Have you told your cacique?"

She pointed to a raised area and said: "Txupira."

It was hard going through the bush. I was wearing Havaiana flip-flops and suddenly felt a deep terror of snakes.

I'd thought we weren't far off and now began to despair as, every time I asked, Naia answered with one finger, pointing to a place always a little farther on.

After some fifteen minutes of pushing on, slipping over, getting up, slipping again, stumbling, our feet continually sinking into the soft muddy ground, we reached the place where Txupira had left Janina, to gather the medicinal plants their mother needed.

Naia told me that Txupira got here through the forest, coming from the other side, a route that would have taken us twice as long.

In the canoe on the way back, concerned about time and the winds bringing more rain, I saw that a section of the vegetation had been crushed.

"Do you often come this way?"

Naia said no. The road was quite close and it scared off their prey.

When we arrived back at the village, almost two hours later, Marcos was worried. Carla was talking to the cacique, explaining that a new jury was going to be selected so Txupira's case could be retried.

"Judge no good thinking," I heard one of them say.

Naia's husband, who couldn't have been more than eighteen, came to meet us. He was not pleased. He pulled the girl to his side and went striding off with her. There was clearly some conflict between them.

I went to the car and toweled off my feet, changed into my spare clothes, combed my hair, and then rejoined the others.

"Where is Naia's house?" I asked one of the boys listening to Carla. He pointed to a hut out to the left.

As I neared it, I heard Naia whimpering. Her husband was doing all the talking: *Zep, zip, ksta, zak,* that knife sound scything through the forest.

I stepped inside without warning. They both turned to look at me, embarrassed.

"I need to talk to you," I said. "Official business."

I stepped outside again and he soon followed me. We walked together as far as the drum full of litter, the central point among all the huts.

"The next time you beat Naia," I said, "I'll be straight back here to arrest you."

He stood there staring at me, stunned.

"We do chemical castrations," I added, smoothly. "You know what that is? Your dick will end up smaller than a cockroach."

We stood in silence, staring at each other.

He asked: "You police?"

"Worse," I replied. "I'm from the League of Women of the Green Stones. And you've been warned."

EPSILON

Bra, life goes on, bra, I walk into the forest, drink the ayahuasca tea, who is this lady rising from the water? *Bra.* This time, garlanded with green stones, her veil a waterfall with electric fish swimming through it. *Bra, life goes on, bra,* I am chewing smoke, dreaming of jaguars, seeing *caiporas* and anacondas, I have guns, I am a vigilante, a heroine without boots, without lipstick, without winged cape but with a holster on my hip, bang-bang, I knock off a few along the way, I am a killer, I am Icamiaba, I am the Amazon, I am the local scourge of sexual terrorists, sexual predators, psycho husbands, neurotic fiancés, and they flee me, they're climbing trees, hiding in bushes, in holes, in burrows, in storm dykes, I go after them, I dig them out, hahahahaha I'm gonna kill Alceu & I'll kill Wendeson & Marcelo & I'll kill my dad & I'll kill Creso & Ermício & Ádila & Alberto, and when they try to shoot me, I'll laugh in their faces, I spew bullets and, deep in the forest here, I walk amid flames, I go deep into the heart of the dream and out the other side, *life goes on,* when I look, it's here in my hands, the green stone with the mysterious key symbol engraved on it, and once more I'm looking at a bunch of keys dangling from the ignition of a car I don't recognize, the keys glint and jingle, I am afraid, I am a child, I'm in the back seat and I can see the dashboard of this strange car with its strange smell, smell of menace, something sour, the radio is on and it's playing the tune *Ob-la-di ob-la-da, life goes on, bra*, and I know that before waking up here, petrified, in this back seat, on the empty highway, I woke up in bed in my dad's new house, in my new bedroom with the mermaid bedspread, I woke on hearing my mother's voice, "Stop it," she was saying, "stop doing this," and I walk barefoot into the corridor and she's here, my mother, beautiful in her dress with the spots, she's here to fetch me, beautiful and frightened, "Go to your room," my father shouts, "Straight to your room," he shouts again, I look at my mother, beautiful and desperate, not knowing this is the last time I'll see her, and from my bed, I hear her sobs, her shouts, her cries for help, doors slamming, and shouts, and help, *terô, terô*, I emerge from the heart of the dream and plunge into the forest, shaken.

"Don't tell me you're crying?" a warrior asks.

"Let her cry," advises another one.

"Dry your tears," commands the Lady of the Green Stones, bringing me a bright cloth scented with frankincense.

I am led back to the lakeside, where a great oven is standing.

Kneeling side by side are Abelardo Ribeiro Maciel and Antônio Francisco Medeiros. There's a sense of euphoria among the warrior women. Some are patently having fun, dancing around the young men with their spears out and chanting:

"U-hu-hi! The men shall die!"

Txupira isn't there. I ask why she's absent.

"It would be like the trial: another rape," one woman explains.

I ask: "How did we catch them?"

"This one we dragged from his bed," another says, pointing at Abelardo.

"And that one was caught on his way out of the house," says another, giving Antônio Francisco a rap on the head.

All the women warriors chant:

"U-hu-hi! The men shall die!"

"Now it's your turn," the Lady of the Green Stones says to me. "How would you like to kill them?"

Before I can answer, the chorus responds.

"We could roast them."

"But first castrate them."

"First we should cut out their tongues."

"I'd like to tear out the guts of one of them with my hands."

Kneeling here, the pair look as though they couldn't kill a fly. But out there in the jungle, with Crisântemo, all three overpowering Txupira, they had called all the shots.

I take out my notebook filled with piles of women and begin to read out the charges.

"When a woman dies, her story must be told and retold a thousand times. Txupira will never again go swimming with Naia. Nor will she sing the songs her grandmother taught her. Txupira will never be a mother, nor will she have grandchildren. Txupira will never see herons again, or curassows or yellow parakeets. She will not eat noodles, which she used to love, on the way home from school. Txupira will never again sleep on her palm-mat floors. Nor will she take Portuguese classes or catch lice from her youngest brother. Someone must pay for this life extinguished."

Abelardo: "Please, think of our mothers, and our families."

The chorus: "Now they want us to think."

Francisco: "We're here to ask for forgiveness."

"We know how that works. First you ask us to forgive you. Then you beat us."

"And then they kill us."

Me: "If you confess to your crime, we'll shoot you from behind. And believe me: it's no fun seeing the bullet coming for you. He who tells you so is your true friend."

The chorus: "The pussy was hers. The guilt is ours. That's the most they can say."

Abelardo: "*Aie, aie*, we already begged to be forgiven! What more can we do?"

Francisco: "We will never again kill anything with a pussy between its legs."

"We are not your evangelical Sunday school class, here to forgive everything, you little bastard!"

"Fourteen, Txupira was only fourteen."

The Lady of the Green Stones: "We must acknowledge: at least they are not here claiming unfitness to comprehend and stand trial, like they do in the white men's trials."

"Or intoxication."

"Who will tell them that round here none of that makes a blind bit of difference?"

"We don't do forgiveness. Or forgetting. Or mercy either."

"What now?" the Lady of the Green Stones asks, turning gently to me. "The manner of the execution will follow your criteria. I could send them to the bottom of the lake. Perhaps you don't feel like having their blood literally on your hands . . . "

"Your shovels," I decide.

Two warriors bring the tools and I hand them to the condemned men. "Dig!" I order.

"Won't there be any trial?" Abelardo asks.

We warrior women laugh heartily at this.

Still they stand there, unmoving, like frightened rabbits.

"You fucking idiot dickheads," I growl. "Get digging!"

The two men obey, miserably, amid prayers; trembling and sobbing, they dig. Francisco mutters, "Lord have mercy," and "Gracious Lady, have pity." Abelardo shits his pants.

The warriors make that sound with their mouths that gives me the shivers: the very note of a knife being sharpened.

The holes are deep and wide. The men are spent.

I pronounce: "If you have anything to say, now is the time."

They begin to weep openly, and to pray.

"I'd like to look away," Abelardo says.

I put a bullet in his forehead.

Francisco makes a break for it; little shit, I almost feel sorry for him. Within seconds the warriors have caught him and set him back down before me. He screws his eyes closed.

I say in my sweetest tone: "Open your eyes, Francisco."

He opens them—well-watered eyes. I squeeze the trigger twice and he falls right into his own hole, just like Abelardo.

Bra. Life goes on.

O

THE DOLL WAS LAUNCHED down the stairs again, making the same great clatter. The recreations of Rita's death scene were building a nervous tension between us. We couldn't relax. With each reenactment, we were reliving the horror.

I'd lost count of how many times Serrano had repeated the scene so he could then analyze the doll's body with minute care. Its weight and measurements matched Rita's precisely. The stairs had been primed with a product that left traces on the doll, which Serrano then compared to the data from the autopsy.

Serrano continued to allow that the body might have been propelled from above, already dead or unconscious at least, unresisting. But he wouldn't rule out the theory of an accident. His process involved a long series of calculations, the results of which he recorded in his notebook. I could see in his concentrated expression just a hint of indignation. "How could they? . . . Idle . . . !" he muttered to himself while scribbling at his clipboard.

His "idlers" were the investigators who had initially established the locus of death. He had only disdain for them. "Were they mad? How could they miss this?" he regularly wondered aloud.

For Carla, who was taking photos, even before the new report reached its conclusion, the outcome was clear.

"These guys are my home-grown Al Capone case," she said of Crisântemo, Abelardo, and Antônio. "If I can't pin Txupira's murder on them, I'll get them for killing Rita."

In fact, the investigators' photos did indicate that Rita had been strangled. However, even with Serrano's initial reports, we didn't have sufficient evidence that Rita's murderers were the same trio who had tortured, raped, and killed Txupira. Besides, Serrano did not believe in the strangling theory, mainly because the official investigators, who were his friends, had confirmed that there was air in Rita's lungs, and this was corroborated by the reports. But Carla refused to give up on her theory, and she missed no opportunity to badmouth Cruzeiro's forensics team, which annoyed Serrano.

"I know what my colleagues have to put up with," he said. "Every Brazilian thinks they can do forensics. Brazilians think they know everything. Brazilians are experts on football and medicine, they know their politics, they're infallible, and they pull rank whenever they can. Brazilians don't play by the rules, they don't stop at traffic lights. When it's time for an impeachment, every Brazilian wants to get in there first—down with the crooks! But directly after, they're off to stand in the disadvantaged line at the bank. Next they're jumping lines at the supermarket. They dodge their taxes; they smoke marijuana all the time. Brazilians really are rotten at heart.

And my poor friends have to pick up the phone when their state representative calls to say, 'There's a body about to come your way and I know you're a good friend, so please, make sure you do this very special corpse first, before the others. And no autopsy!' That's Brazilians for you. You have to keep on explaining: even representatives, violent deaths, suspected violent deaths—every one of them has to be autopsied! You're not the one signing the papers, am I right? So let me do my work in peace."

And then Carla was rash enough to praise the work of forensic investigators in São Paulo.

"Don't try telling me about São Paulo!" Serrano shot back. "I've seen a Paulista investigator photographing people who were still alive, thinking they were corpses. And there's worse. Down there, soon as you're dead, you're ripe for exploitation. Everyone and their dog gets a bite of you. It's only us, the forensics, who get nothing, because dead people don't tip. We get left with the bad rep. Know why? Take a trip to the São Paulo morgue and you'll see how their system works. The funeral directors, everyone on their way out of the prison system, they're all hanging around the corridors extorting the hell out of the bereaved relatives. They don't even properly cover their tracks. They go up to the deceased's father or mother or brother and feed them barefaced lies: 'Your dead relative will rot from waiting so long. But if you give me this money, I'll get them to release the body right away.' The terrified relative gives even more than they can afford. And *we* get the reputation for corruption—that's São Paulo for you."

For the duration of his rants, Serrano neglected his tasks, or perhaps he simply forgot about the doll and the notes that needed taking. Denis, who was keeping track of the cost of the forensic investigations, was stumped as to how to speed him up.

"Don't chat with him," he told Carla, privately. "Let the guy get on with it."

Marcos filmed the whole process, at the forensic expert's request, for he would later make the footage part of yet another report to add to the inquiry.

My role here, along with Denis, was to scour the house for something, we had no idea what: something that would in some way correspond to the information Rita had mentioned in her last phone call to Carla.

"It could be a piece of paper, an electronic file, a letter, a photo . . ." Carla reminded us. "I'm guessing it's some information about Txupira's death—that was all we were talking about before Rita died."

We did a thorough clean-out of the drawers in the living room, the kitchen, and the dining room. As with any journalist, the quantity of paper and notebooks Rita had accumulated was immense, so this was not a small undertaking.

"Time out?" Denis asked. He had disappeared for a moment and now returned to the living room carrying freshly brewed coffee. The smell of it filled the air.

It was only that morning, as we chatted while Serrano worked, that I realized Carla and Denis were having an affair.

"Test drive," she said to me later, at last revealing the reason for her abrupt lack of interest in Paulo. "There's one good thing about this relationship, besides the sex. Denis lives in a different city. He doesn't hang around, doesn't cling to me like Paulo."

After many measurements and reruns, Serrano was still doubtful as to whether the brain hemorrhage that killed Rita was caused by an accident on the stairs.

"If it was a fall, the body would have undergone a much greater kinetic impact, and the fracture would have been quite different," he insisted.

But it all looked different by the end of the afternoon, once he'd made a more thorough sweep of the interior walls.

"I need a longer ladder."

Denis borrowed one from a neighbor.

Serrano raised it in the hallway of the upper floor; from there he was able to examine the ceiling. "Is there any way we can make it dark up here?" he asked.

Marcos and Carla closed all the windows and doors on the ground floor and Denis and I did the same for all the bedrooms.

Serrano took a product from his case and sprayed it over the ceiling. Then we saw what he'd been looking for: a few spatters of blood.

"If that's Rita's," he said, "someone'll have to explain how it got all the way up here."

Denis closed his eyes. Carla squeezed his hand. Serrano said: "If she had fallen, her blood could not have reached the ceiling. Of that I can assure you."

Dammit, my darling, what a shitshow!

At this juncture, Marcos went off to look after a horse at a ranch outside Cruzeiro and Denis flew back to Rio Branco. Carla and I left to eat a plate of *tambaqui* fish ribs in a restaurant by the central market. We were famished, tired, and stressed.

If you need me, I'm here!

Carla had slept through almost our entire journey home from the Kuratawa village the day before. So it was only over dinner, after sitting back with a glass of beer, that I was able to tell her about my trip into the forest with Naia, to where Txupira had last been seen.

How about a threesome with a lorry driver—does that make you wet?

"It didn't look as though no one ever went there," I said. "The opposite, actually. The vegetation had been trampled in several places."

"There are people who trespass in the designated territories. Fishing, hunting, stealing timber. It's quite common, unfortunately," Carla said.

"There's no game to hunt there because of the highway," I said. "If they're trespassing, it must be for some other reason."

Carla didn't see much value in my story. *I'll fuck you in every hole.* The trampling was recent. How could it have anything to do with Txupira's death? Besides, she had no data on this place in the legal proceedings.

What did catch her attention was my story of the grilling I'd given Naia's husband.

"The situation is much more complicated than you think," she said. "These people have their own systems, their own ways of resolving misbehavior within the community."

"She's pregnant! What if she miscarries because he's beaten her?"

"Lots of the women are beaten. There's a strong sense of patriarchy and machismo among the indigenous people. But you behaved as if you were in Cruzeiro do Sul—or São Paulo. You don't know anything about these people."

"What do you think I should have done—sat tight?"

"What I can say for sure is that the Maria da Penha Law doesn't fix anything around here. It's just for white women, urban women. If we wanted to protect Naia we'd have to talk about indigenous land demarcation. The more vulnerable the community, the more lacking in infrastructure, the more indigenous women live with this kind of violence, which is, really, collateral damage from the way indigenous people are treated everywhere in Brazil. Look, I'm not criticizing you. I've also interfered in situations like that. Want to know what one woman who was assaulted said? 'Let him beat me. It's my body. He enjoys it.'"

Carla had been working in Acre for nearly four years. She clearly had an understanding of the situation that I couldn't grasp at all. What she meant was that our institutions were not built with the indigenous people in mind.

"As recently as seventy years ago, they were slaves on this land," she said. "Indigenous people are not invisible in our society the way Black people can be. That's not what we're talking about. It's different—it's a wholly other situation. They simply don't exist. They were decimated; they're still being decimated. Take a look at the stats at the Ministry for Racial Equality: there isn't a single policy for indigenous people. They simply don't belong to our society—they don't exist. This is why Txupira's death is all the more unacceptable. They killed a unicorn."

Of my stay in Cruzeiro do Sul, of all that was engraved in my memory of the tragedy that overwhelmed us after that day, the clearest image I retain is of Carla explaining the death of the unicorn. By this point, I had already reached the heart of the jungle, I had drunk ayahuasca, I had felt that glow in my skin after bathing in the river, I had danced with my bare feet on the earth and smelled the fragrance of that half-lit natural world which is always growing, miraculously sprouting, flowering, dying, and being reborn before our eyes. I had seen the plastic flowers in Txupira's mother's hut; I had received my green stone from the hands of the Lady of the Green Stones; I had witnessed the wild strength and joy of Zapira's maloca, and also the debasement of the Kuratawa, such that I'd gone home thinking that I, a person of the South, of tarmacked streets and the twenty-first century, of the country without a future, I had finally encountered the unicorn Carla was talking about.

I remember now my tangible sense of privilege, being able to go back to my house. On the way, I saw that Bia had called me several times. I was also intrigued by a series of strange messages from friends and ex-colleagues and even more from people I didn't know, all of the latter wildly insulting. They couldn't be meant for me.

I called Bia back.

"What's going on?"

"Better talk to Denise," she said.

"What should I say?"

Denise couldn't sack me twice, I thought.

"She said you should call her—right away," Bia said again.

I did as Bia suggested.

"Your report is outstanding," Denise said, when she picked up.

In the silence that followed, it felt as though someone must have died. I had a powerful urge to hang up and call my grandma.

Then Denise told me. She'd been deeply shocked: the office had received some videos that included images of me—intimate images, showing me naked, me having sex.

Even before I saw the images, I knew this could only be Amir's work.

"They have a name for this in America: 'revenge porn,'" Denise said.

"Could you send it to me?" I asked.

That was the first time I think I really understood the meaning of sisterly solidarity.

"There are two things I have to say," Denise said before we hung up. "First: I'll defend you in this case, pro bono. It's never easy but sometimes we manage to bring an asshole like this one before a judge. I'll need help from your end too, of course. Second: I don't want to know, unless you want to tell me, why it was that you vanished and left me in the dark. I guess you're going through a difficult time. So, I want you to know that, when you're ready, the doors of this office are wide open for you to come back. I really want you back working with us."

I truly didn't know what to say. Nor do I remember how the call ended.

What I remember is sitting on my veranda looking at the filth Denise had sent me. In one of the photos, I was sitting on the toilet, naked, cutting my right toenails, without any knickers. Of them all, that was the only one that had been taken with my consent. I even remember what Amir had said then—that I was beautiful, even on the toilet. Even taking a shit. Even menstruating. The others had been taken without permission. Scenes of us screwing. How had he recorded them without me knowing? In another video, I was in the shower, washing my bottom. It was unbelievable.

Later I found out that Amir had also sent the photos to a site that enabled anonymous uploads of pornographic material. The captions managed to be even worse than the images: "Criminal lawyer, modern woman, no hang-ups. I love group sex." Worst of all, he had included my phone number. The messages would not stop. *I'll suck you till you scream. Lush. Pretty little tart. Come to my house. Do you like it up the ass too? Come and suck my dick.*

Suddenly, amid a violent wave of nausea, I understood what was happening. I was being burned alive like a witch, with the whole world watching. Since he was unable to kill me physically, that utter scum Amir was trying to burn me on a virtual pyre.

10

KILLED OVER A VIDEO GAME

Taita Gomes was in the kitchen at home
when her husband came in
and found their nine-year-old son
playing a video game,
something he had banned
completely.
"Video games only when I allow them," he had said.
Gripping the boy
with one hand
and his gun with the other,
her husband went into the kitchen and shot his wife in the head,
saying afterwards to his son:
"That'll teach you
never to disobey me again."

P

"ARE YOUR EARS HUMMING?" Zapira asked.

Sitting under the samaúma tree, legs crossed and eyes closed, I could hardly feel my ears at all. Beyond the leafy canopy, a powerful sun was shining in an azure sky. A soft wind lifted my hair. With both hands held like a shell around her mouth, Zapira blew into my face: *fuhshuhsuhsuh*. The tobacco smoke floated softly around my thoughts.

"Tunki, tunki, tunki," she sang, explaining that "tunki" is "the vulture king who devours spells, sicknesses, and wickedness."

I was also given a new name: Rawa-kah—warm breeze, in Zapira's language. "To complete the *puçanga*," she said. Some evil enchantment had been thrown, or spat, or blown over my name, and that was why I was in a slow decline, and death was little by little eating me away, she explained.

"Now the evil will go," she said. "Keep your new name; it's not for using, it's for keeping. Protect your name, don't say it aloud. Whoever knows our name knows how to hurt us."

Zapira herself had prepared the genipap dye that lay ready in a ceramic pot beside us. It had taken eight days: she first picked the fruit and then grated it until it oozed the greenish juice she was now spreading over my body.

Using a strip of palm leaf, Zapira drew a line along my body, then another. One opening up, another closing. Fine, continuous, precise; her strokes radiated out obliquely from a central point on my forehead and rose up to the sky, leaving my body, extending me into space, beyond myself.

"You're growing very tall," Zapira said, laughing.

The children were skulking around us. Come, come here, come, Zapira said to them. Another line, and another. This one joining up with that, beginning here, finishing there. *Whap*, one of the kids tapped me on the back, killing a mosquito. *Whop*, another tap, another insect swatted.

It was Marcos who'd dragged me out of bed and taken me to Zapira's village, so she could paint my body with genipap.

Wounded, I had been crawling through my personal Via Crucis over and over, alone at home for days and nights, sick of life, bone-weary in bed, so fucking sick, in a fetal position, shaking with revulsion in my dark bedroom, swearing, kicking out, whimpering, howling like a wolf, really so fucking crushed. Amir's little movie special was all I could think about, rerunning it from start to finish and over again, my tits in close-up & my vagina cutting my nails & my ass mid-ablution & our coitus uncut & the black strips across the offender's eyes & everything online, available, multiplying like a deadly epidemic at incredible speed, feeding a chain of idiots, all of them laughing at me, all jerking off at me with my legs apart & me sucking & me licking & me being licked & me coming & just thinking about the comments—yes, I had made the mistake of reading the comments by consumers of this homemade porn, porn made by my former boyfriend without my knowledge, without my desire to be filmed, knife-in-the-back porn: "I know just what to do with sluts like you," wrote one, "Oh how I'd like to set that pussy on fire," wrote another, "We so gagin (sic) for free pussys (sic)" wrote this one, "Put a sign on your pussy sayin 'new management' n come round my pad so I can induct my new screw," wrote that one. The comments alone were enough to cry about for the rest of my life, to cry until I dissolved and could flow down my sheets, take refuge in the middle of the mattress foam and live in there, dried out, forever, like urine spilled from a body that's lost control, no strength for anything, no heart for anything, no heart to answer the phone, Hi Denise, yes Denise, I'm listening, Put it on paper now, says Denise, this isn't a request, it's an order, I don't know if I want to prosecute Amir, I answer, Get out of bed right now and put it all down on paper, she orders, and send me all of Amir's details, I want to know everything about that piece of shit, postcode, ID number, address, his routine, his work, his favorite bars, names of his friends, the works, and I obeyed, I wrote down everything for her, then I went back to bed and slept, I signed the power of attorney and back to bed, to cry, I couldn't face showing up for the trial, couldn't face being out in public, but Bia said: Don't be daft! & my grandma said: If you don't prosecute, I'll do something much worse & Marcos said: Zapira knows some excellent ways to get people out of bed, come with me, and me with my last thread of strength, the strength just to sleep and live here, in my hole, burrowed deep inside my mattress like dried urine, living off the foam and, over time, dissolving into dust.

In a way, online death is more perverse than real-life death. It is the dead you that has to deal with the fallout from your ongoing life. It's you who has to navigate the administrative process. I couldn't bring myself to deal with it. So Marcos pulled me out of bed and bundled me into the car, "Dammit, princess, let's go paint your body," he said, and on the way he told me about the first time he'd had his body painted. "You only get what it means to be part of this planet when your body is painted," he said. "When they painted my body I understood what they meant by coming from dust and returning to dust. When they painted me, I was catapulted back into my heritage, I was crazy just to get out there and hunt jaguar," he said, adding that before being painted, his spirit had been hurting, "and it wasn't a small pain, it hurt so much, it hurt and it bled." He gripped my hand tightly. "You're going to be okay."

And then—now—I was there, surrounded by children, beneath the samaúma, with triangles drawn point-to-point over my arms and legs, and hexagons and quadrilaterals, which linked into labyrinths—possibilities—traps—pathways. Where the enemy can enter, Zapira explained. It was here, in these labyrinths, that the evil would lose its way, she said.

Before being painted, I was washed in a wooden trough, in an infusion of fifteen different herbs as well as tobacco. Then I was given a spear for hunting tapirs, with a poisoned tip. Zapira blew snuff into my right nostril. Then into the left. "It must be in both nostrils," Marcos explained later. "Otherwise it might cause an imbalance in your brain."

I didn't recognize myself in the paint. I don't know if that was when I stopped dying. What I know is that while I was helping the village women to collect honey in the forest, I decided to turn my notebook of dead women into a public website that would also include a description of what had happened to me. I decided to personally repost the images he'd already released anonymously, the same pornographic stuff, except that here, on my own web pages, within my own website, my vagina, me cutting my nails, all the hundreds of pictures of pussy and ass and sex with Amir's face blacked out and mine in close-up would not be exposing me—it would expose him and every man like him. These pages would be my vaccine. I would use Amir's virus to inoculate myself against the disease of Amir. My virtual pages would be the perfect counterattack, an exemplary battlefield riposte, the very model of online assassination by an ex, a project I would follow through to the end.

That night we sat around the bonfire eating sweet manioc and banana. I was still clinging to my tapir spear. We slept in hammocks in Zapira's maloca and awoke to voices singing about the Lord and rising to the heavens and sins and demons.

On the way back to Cruzeiro do Sul, I asked Marcos about the singing and learned that there was actually a pastor in the community, and that many of the indigenous people were evangelical Christians.

"You don't know these people. They're not doing the aya-huasca rituals," he said.

"But they're indigenous people?" I asked.

"Of course," Marcos replied.

"How do Zapira and the other indigenous people who maintain their community traditions live alongside the evangelicals?"

So Marcos told me his people's story.

"You need to understand that a lot of blood has been spilled here. As they say: even more blood than rubber. Of the eight hundred Ch'aska who used to make up the community, by the time of the second rubber boom, there were only fifty-seven left. They lost everything: land as well as culture. Do you know what it means to lose your own language? The rubber bosses made it illegal for my grandparents to speak their own language."

Marcos explained that the people who were now living in the Ch'aska village were the children, grandchildren, and great-grandchildren of those fifty-seven. They had lived for decades in absolute misery—and, at a certain point, they had turned to the evangelical church. Then, many of the women began losing their babies shortly after they were born. Many: first one, then three, six, then fifteen. Mothers in the village wept and screamed, some threw themselves into the river, hoping to die, too. So Zapira's father started to visit other communities; he told them about the dying babies and the pajés of these communities came to visit the Ch'aska to try to understand what was happening. They tried everything: all the herbs, all the roots, all the vines, all the chants, all the buds, all the rituals, all the dances, and—according to Marcos—there was not one herb or ritual or dance from this or that community or from this or that pajé that could end the curse of the stillborn babies. Ultimately, although the community believed that using the yellow frog's poison was what eradicated the curse, "What stopped the cycle of death was the rebirth of the community as a people of the forest, with its beliefs, its language, and its own culture," Marcos explained—and now I saw that there were some ways the unicorn might live again.

All of this revived my strength and energy. Back home, I already had several plans. Arrows! Fire. I would speak to Denise. Gunpowder. To my grandmother. Poisoned darts. To Bia. Spears. I would assemble data. Ordnance. The war was on. thesimpleartofkillingawoman.com.

But first, I went to my room and, without opening the shutters, took off my clothes and stared carefully at my painted body in the mirror. *Rawa-kah*, I said, softly. It was as if I were a new species, a new creature. My skin had become snakelike, covered in paths and labyrinths and triangles that linked together, with lines running here and there, up and down, making me genuinely dizzy. I sat on the bed and a broad sensation of peace came over me. I felt my heart beating through all my cells. My eyes were two birds ready to take off. *Flap, flap, flap.*

I woke up on the sofa, fully clothed, with my phone ringing.

"Where did you go?" asked Carla, sounding upset.

"What time is it?" I asked.

"Eleven."

I was confused. I'd arrived home at midday.

"At night?" I asked, surprised that I could have slept through the whole afternoon.

"Are you wasted? It's eleven in the morning."

I had slept for almost twenty-four hours.

Carla said, "You need to get over here now. We need to come up with a plan. I'm frightened. I admit it. I really am."

"What's happened?"

"You don't know?" she asked.

Her tone was panicked.

"Txupira's murderers were killed last night," she said. "A total slaughter. They killed all three of them."

ZETA

They were saying: You like *inhambu*? You like spider monkey? Kill a peccary, lady! Hook a catfish. Slather yourself in açaí. Eat bacuri berries. You want white yam? Come over here to the plantings. Pick cassava or yams or pumpkins. Over there are chestnuts and *murici*. Do you like peach-palm? We have piquiá and *tatu*, and you can hunt *jacu*. Kill a deer. Eat *pitanga* and *camutim*. You don't want graviola?

Shshoooo, I blew out. Not even nauseous. No way. Shshshoooooo. Do they think I'm an idiot?

The voices coming from the forest were as various as the things they were offering. Try *guariba* monkey, they said. Taste our honey. Try trumpeter birds. They could offer me the heavens and the Earth, our menu was ready to go. And no stern reproof can frighten a warrior woman. We were famished. "Today we shall eat until our asses rebel," the Lady of the Green Stones said, preparing the fire. It would be a great feast, I knew. I invited Rusyleid & Iza & Silvana & Regina & Ketlen & Soraia and lots more. The whole gang from A to Z.

With my flaming torch and my cudgel, making my way between the giants of the jungle, I had no trouble recognizing or plucking the tannia leaves. This is what happens when your

174

body is painted, I thought: everything that was tangled untangles. Everything that was slow speeds up. What was invisible becomes visible. What had stopped starts to move. What was moving forward comes racing back. What had been prey becomes the hunter.

It was a red-letter day. I felt like a hundred-year-old samaúma, surrounded by parakeets and toucans. It's one thing to be a tall woman, and another to be a tall tree, the Lady of the Green Stones had said. Like in that poem, I thought: growing for ages, not hurting anyone. What was this strength—where had it come from? From the upside-down triangles gleaming on my arms? Hahahaha, colored in with the genipap dye, I had crossed a line. I'd gone over the edge. Now, yes, it was possible to speak with smoke. With the forest's spirits. Where are the talking jaguars? I wondered, looking around.

I came flying back over the treetops, astride my torch the way witches mount their broomsticks, the flame burning behind with me in front. At the lake, the warriors were waiting for me. Hanging from the tree trunks, like flags, and spread out on the grass around the fire, were the many multicolored cloths that decorated our maloca. Oh, how delightful! The ground had been swept with *titica* vines. Someone had brought banana wine. And there were many fruits: *mari, patauá,* mangos, oranges, but this was for afterwards. The sweet manioc was boiled, stamped down, chewed, spat out, and sweetened with honey to make *caiçuma,* to moisten a dry mouth.

This time, none of the *Ob-la-di, ob-la-da.* None of the *terô, terô.* Just *batuque* drums, smoke, rhythm, tall *atabaque* drums, and chants of revenge. Without revenge, we cannot forget.

Seeing me, the women began to lick their lips.

"The meat smells good," one called out.

Over the fire stood a great cauldron, full and bubbling. In the stew were all the meats. Also chilies and a dash of *tucupi*, another of paracress, and some chicory.

"Where's the tannia?"

I pointed to the leaves I had just gathered in the jungle. They were thrown into the pot.

Mix well. Add water. Scatter chili and cumaru and mastic. Let it boil. Boil through the day and boil through the night. The sun rises and sets. We sing and we dance. We see the grass grow.

The atabaques herald them.

At last Txupira comes with her people. They come, hollering and pointing their guns, to join the celebration. It's our way of remembering those who have died, from A to Z. And it's a warning: here we don't play games about killing. Revenge feared is a lesson learned.

Afterwards we take snuff and gossip and laugh. Some of the women go swimming. Others just want to drink and dance and recite sacred poems. Czesław Miłosz: "Change into a tree, grow for ages, not hurt anyone." Many of the women settle beneath the trees and chat about someone they know, a neighbor, a sister, a friend, a cousin, a sister-in-law, an unhappy woman, about themselves or others, nameless women, who unwittingly found themselves turned into an object. Into a demon. Into a body. Into a clothes hanger. Into market appeal. Into a prostitute. Into a punchbag. Into a worthless thing. Into a domestic slave. Into a hole. Into a retail platform. Into a sex toy. Into a cow.

"I never heard anyone talk about a holy pussy," one of them says.

It's time to eat. We lick our lips and salivate.

One of the warriors brings *aninga* leaves for us to use as plates. And one by one, the women speak up.

"Abelardo's leg is mine."

"I could share Antônio's ribs with someone."

We have shaved the two murderers' heads and washed and skinned their bodies. With our long knives, we have carefully dismembered them, stripping away the viscera, which we washed in the river and dried on the ground.

"We have two heads. Here is abundance!"

"Now we can make an animal—with four legs."

"And four arms."

"And two torsos," I add.

"This is for you," says the Lady of the Green Stones, presenting pieces of meat to Txupira. (Her pussy no longer sports the black censoring strip—and now she's getting compliments: ah, what a beautiful vagina!) They are the men's private parts. More than anyone here, she deserves to put an end to them. Generously, Txupira proposes to share the delicacies with me.

But I choose Antônio's heart. In the end, he and Abelardo were lucky, I think while chewing; luckier than Crisântemo. In the end, both could have been food for the worms, like Crisântemo, but instead they ended up in our cooking pot.

We burn everything that was theirs: their bloody clothes, their memories, their shoes, their belts, their intentions, their hats, their wallets, their hair, their thoughts, their ID papers. Now they can't drag us with them to the land of the dead, nor be tempted to stay among us, like shades. We burn their bones down, too, grind them to powder and add them to the banana wine and fermented caiçuma, which we drink until it almost knocks us out.

I am practically asleep when the Lady of the Green Stones tugs at my hand.

"The time has come," she says. "I'm taking you to a special place."

We rise through the dark trees, skimming low, then rising again, flying over the treetops, circling like vultures, gliding into the heart of the forest, and there below is the throbbing jungle, great volumes of racing waters, feathers and fur and sharp teeth, wild creatures and their prey, some hunting and others hunted, some eating and others eaten, humble souls, hungry souls, poor communities, and others poorer still. Is there gold? Yes: there are bone-dry seeds, soy, cattle, drought, agro-toxins, and bad people; we fly lower, feeling the breeze on our faces, the smoke from burn-off, such grief, and here is a felled strip, here another stretch bare of trees, and then more, the biggest clearance, and then huge stretches of burned earth, some trees chopped to the ground, others simply burned down, and vast farms, so much soy and cattle, and here a chainsaw, a tractor, a digger, another saw, oh the terror, Tim-berrrrrrr! One tree falls and ten fall and a hundred fall and two thousand are falling, and here trespassers, here loggers, what a shame. And here a clandestine airstrip in action, we fly faster, here another secret airstrip, right here, and more pneumatic drills, tractors, diggers. Oh the fear and people digging and people burning the bush, and farther ahead an ugly town, beauty has retreated somewhere else, beyond it, hiding in the heart of the forest, while beneath us there is nothing but sad dust yards, fences, traffic jams, unemployment, floods, apathy, abandoned schools, abandoned peoples, black smoke, abandoned museums, abandoned libraries, oh the desolation! And we swing with the wind, let it blow us high above and, even so, even through the black cloud sweating over the city, we can still see the men in suits down there, it makes my stomach heave, we fly lower, so many stupid people and crooked people and truly rotten people. "Look there's Guanabara Bay," I say, and we glide on, till we're nearing São Paulo, over a highway racked with bends and the odd plantation, bends to right and left, and more bends, and so we whirl onwards, bound for the mountains.

"Do you remember this place?" asks the Lady of the Green Stones, pointing to a valley below that is dotted with purple glory trees. It seems there are so many stories to remember that I can't recall anything about here. Holding the other's hand, we come down into the valley alongside a crashed vehicle. A rollover. A woman's arm dangles out of a window.

As I land, I see that it's my mother lying dead in the driver's seat.

"Now tell me," says the Lady of the Green Stones, letting my hand go. "How did she end up here?"

We stand there, looking at my mother. Even dead, she is still beautiful.

Q

AFTER A SHORT BREAK, the judge limped in. One of his shoes was a moccasin, the other a leather sandal. His big toe was wrapped in gauze and looked to be the size of an egg. During the hearing, he allowed the sandal to slip off and sat there massaging and caressing the injured foot. An ingrown nail, I learned later.

"Sometimes you feel as if it's all a waste of time," the caseworker standing outside had said. He let me bum a cigarette. He was very thin, a pipecleaner of a man. "And so the weeks roll by—fly by—carrying us toward death." He gazed thoughtfully into the middle distance. In the square before us, the treetops had been pruned into geometric shapes, as if the residents wanted to show the indomitable force of nature around them who was boss here. We smoked in silence.

"Have you seen how it goes?" he asked, at last looking me in the eye. "At the trial, the girl says she was raped. Then she comes here and says no, actually, she only said that because she was fed up with her boyfriend. In the end, accused and victim walk out of here holding hands."

A silence.

"I shouldn't be working so much," he said, and ground out his cigarette under a cheap heel. Before we went in, he offered me a banana he had brought from home. "I'm not hungry," he said, offering his own conclusion.

It was chilly inside the courtroom, even after they turned off the air-conditioning. The chamber was almost empty. I saw only the minimum staff, the thin caseworker and a couple more people who went in and out. By three in the afternoon, nobody had yet stopped for lunch. Everyone was living on bananas, biscuits, and coffee brought from home. They called the aggressor and victim for the next case but neither appeared. The defending counsel made the routine speech required by protocol. Defendant condemned. One hearing after another, at industrial pace. "He shoved me and called me a whore," the victim said. Carla looked exhausted. Public prosecutor, public defender, defendant, accused, all involved in this decision: did he or did he not push her? The accused admitted he did push her; he was drunk.

"But it was only a tiny tap, she's exaggerating."

"Exaggerating? You broke my arm!"

"Are you still drinking?" Carla asked the kid defendant.

"Yes."

"Every day?"

"Yes."

"Then you have a problem," she said. "Will you accept social assistance?"

"Yes I will. Thank you so much."

The thin man sighed.

I had to watch the proceedings of two further cases before Carla was done for the day. In a way, it was frightening how the court went on with its work. In the last few days, with the deaths of Crisântemo, Abelardo, and Francisco, it seemed the whole city had come to a halt. In the bars, in the park, where little kids scattered bread for the alligators, in the restaurants, at bus stops, in the malls, around the creeks, in the central market, and in the forest, there was no other topic of conversation. A wave of rebellion and indignation was sweeping the city. So young, they protested as one voice. So handsome. Their lives ahead of them. Such cruelty! Such barbarism! Where will the murdering end? This was the question on everybody's lips. The streets and houses where the young men had lived were full of friends, acquaintances, busybodies, journalists, investigators, and police officers.

The three memorial services emptied the streets of Cruzeiro do Sul. The city filled with banners proclaiming *Crisântemo—present! Abelardo—present! Francisco—present!* I could hardly believe it when I saw them. In fact, in the midst of my fury, I had a fit of giggles. I thought about making my own that read: *Rapist—present! Murderers—present!* All of a sudden, and solely because they were dead, because they'd each gone down with a bullet to the head, the men were apparently cleared of Txupira's murder. Their obituaries might have been written about a trio of saints. Students, good sons, good citizens, good families— that's what filled the newspapers. Good families! The mayor announced three days of mourning. "We will not accept this violence. These young people's deaths will not go unpunished," he thundered to the press. There was no one in the city or even anywhere in the state who had not, by this time, seen images of the boys' mothers at the funeral ceremonies, one of them in a faint, another hysterical, the third visibly tranquilized. Each one supported on all sides.

The whole police machine was mobilized for the investigation. The boys' bodies had been found on the shores of the Juruá river in a stretch of dense forest, not far from where they had dumped Txupira's lifeless body. But nobody mentioned that. What's more, Txupira's name was suddenly taboo. "You want to trample on their graves?" asked the manager of the petrol station where I refilled my car. "The boys are dead. What good can it do now to ask whether or not they killed the Indian girl?"

The forensics' consensus was that the boys were killed in the place where they were found. The shots had been fired a short distance, by a single gun, which meant that one boy had had the bad luck of seeing the other two die before him.

While I waited for Carla to finish her tasks at the courthouse, I read in the *Caderno do Acre* that Crisântemo had received a call from a public phone booth two hours before his death. According to the police, this phone call was the key that would unlock the crime.

The night before, I'd had dinner with Carla, Denis, and Marcos, and was surprised to learn that Carla had been called to testify.

"Do they think you killed our assassins?" I asked, teasing.

"Denis has been called too," she said.

"It's to be expected," Denis added. "You'll be subpoenaed too. Everyone who was involved in Txupira's case, in whatever way, will get a summons."

"Me?" I was shocked.

"If you want to understand the significance of these boys' deaths, you need first to understand 'the Acre question,'" Denis said. "These playboys were not only three wealthy scions of the city. They were great- and great-great-grandsons of Acre's founders, of the people who were driven here by the great drought in Ceará state, in the North-East—I mean at the end of the nineteenth century, when this region still belonged to Bolivia and was known as uncharted land. With their machetes and their mirrors, their clothes and other trinkets, these people hoodwinked the indigenous community, who had always been here and who were the true owners of this vast jungle. They ejected, killed, or enslaved the indigenous people and set themselves up as major rubber barons. And when Bolivia began to seek ways of reaching the Atlantic to get rid of the junk it was producing, or worse, when it began negotiating with the United States to lease out this land for rubber exploitation—rubber being the ultimate raw material of their modern times—Brazil's self-styled rubber barons were incensed. At the time, they'd just gone through a period of vast bloodshed, they'd killed thousands and thousands of indigenous people, so the idea of moving on to kill Bolivians shocked no one. The 'Acre question' prompted them to organize, to put together troops—troops of poets, madmen, lawyers, doctors, indigenous people, journalists, actual soldiers—whoever they could convince by whipping, paying, or appealing to patriotism. There were years of struggle. They made losses and gains. And more losses. The Acre question became a national question and then an international one. Eventually they declared Acre an independent state. A Spanish journalist called Galvez, who had discovered and exposed the story of the Bolivian Syndicate, the first international intervention in Amazonia, became the biggest leader of this new state—but Brazil still would not recognize it. Worse still: Acre was then invaded by the Brazilian navy and returned to Bolivia. It was like an appalling joke. It was thanks to these men, to these killers of the indigenous people, thanks to their money, that the Baron of Rio Branco sat down at the negotiating table with the Bolivians and bought Acre for two million pounds sterling. And ever since, these men and their descendants rule and overrule in these parts. They own almost all the places where you can buy things you'll need. They lost a lot through the demarcation of indigenous territories. But they still have the cities. The three boys who died are blood relatives of these people."

This was what was worrying Carla: once again the indigenous people were taking the hit. What she saw, reading between the lines of news reports, conversations overheard at the courthouse, and the investigators' posturing, was a general inclination to blame the boys' crimes on the Kuratawa people.

"Look at this," she said, taking from her handbag a copy of the *Terra Nova* paper—whose owner was uncle to one of the boys. She read: "'These murders are the actions of communist Indian-worshippers,'"—and, indignant, repeated, "communist Indian-worshippers!'" She rolled her eyes. "I ask you!"

So that day, after the court had closed, we went to Txupira's village. Carla wanted to explain what was going on to the people there—to alert them to the risks of violence. She had already sent a warning to the National Indian Foundation, and was hoping they would now be in touch with Brazil's Institute of the Environment and Renewable Natural Resources. And then, hopefully, they would do something about it.

"But I don't hold out much hope. We're living in a new era," she said as we turned onto the highway. "The old families never accepted the demarcation of the indigenous territories. Now they feel justified going into the communities and threatening the inhabitants."

Carla was not particularly disturbed by the boys' having been murdered. She was, though, concerned that the Kuratawa might become the new target. And how on earth had she not managed to bring down Txupira's murderers?

Like everyone else, I was moved by the pain of the victims' mothers. I never could handle seeing a mother cry. But that was it: there ended my sympathy. Their deaths did not affect me. Yes, the boys had had their lives ahead of them. So had Txupira. They had been killed in a cruel way. So had Txupira. Actually, they'd suffered less than she had. They'd been luckier. They hadn't been raped with a whisky bottle.

Unlike Carla, I hadn't the slightest illusion that, had they remained alive, the boys would have finished their days in jail. That could not have happened—ever. Not in Brazil. They'd have wriggled out of it somehow. In truth, I was relieved they were dead, and said so to Carla.

"Do not say that in front of other lawyers," she warned.

"I can't do forgiveness," I confessed. "To me, forgiveness is revenge in a lead and collar. Revenge repressed."

Carla stared at me. "Are you serious?"

"Some crimes can't be forgiven."

"Really?"

"Who killed Rita? Who killed Txupira?" I asked.

"I'll ask again: Are you serious? Because, right now, you've got us talking about the death penalty. I don't want to discover you're a supporter of the death penalty."

"Of course I'm not. I just can't be sorry that they died."

"Should I be asking where you were on the night Txupira's murderers were murdered?"

We laughed.

By the time we reached Txupira's village, I was feeling off-color. I couldn't suppress the shivers occasionally running through me, despite the heat outside.

"If they come, we will fight," the cacique said, on hearing what was happening. I looked around at the people gathered around their leader, standing, leaning against trees, or squatting or sitting on the ground, so dispossessed, their arms crossed, hands held in their armpits, listening hard despite the fierce heat, surrounded by garbage, by plastic, tin cans. I could not picture them resisting. They looked like victims, like cattle on their way to the abattoir. Flies hummed around us.

Then Txupira's mother began to speak. We couldn't understand what she was saying. She spoke without a pause, in a monotone. The men began to argue among themselves, but

Txupira's mother talked on, ignoring them. Gradually, they fell silent. Carla asked for someone to translate.

The cacique closed his eyes and began. He said the old lady assured us it was she who killed the boys, by means of witchcraft. That Txupira had come to her in a dream and asked her to do it. That in her dream, Txupira had ordered her to catch a yellow macaw and pluck out its feathers, to collect honey from wild bees, and to cut down green branches from a wild lemon tree. And to find some cipó vine—good, strong lengths. That on the night of the full moon, she should bring all of this with her, and go alone. That was important. No man must see her. Arriving in the middle of the jungle, she had to create a platform using the lime tree branches, securing its corners with the vine. Then decorate her structure with the macaw feathers and put the good sweet honey inside it. She had to dig three holes beside this structure, one hole for each murderer, and lean down into each one and shout their names, three times. She had done all of this to the letter, then made her way back to the maloca without anyone seeing her. She awoke with Txupira whispering in her ear to turn on the radio. And when she did, she heard the news that the boys were dead. This was her spell.

When she'd finished, the old lady turned around and walked away. From where we stood, we could see her hanging clean clothes on a washing line stretched between trees in the clearing. T-shirts, shorts, and dresses, their colors slightly revived by the water, but all ragged, torn, filled with holes.

Carla suggested they strengthen their vigilance over their lands for the next while.

As we were getting back into the car to return to Cruzeiro, Naia came running up to me. Her belly was a little bigger and she looked happy. She gave me a necklace of yellow beads.

"I made it," she said, putting them around my neck. Her bare arms were clear of bruises.

11

THE SIMPLE ART OF KILLING A WOMAN

On Monday
the murderer took from the fridge
a bottle of water,
the pasta left over
from Sunday's
lunch or dinner,
the black bean stew
as yet unseasoned
for the week,
or perhaps the wrinkled tomatoes and lettuce
for his salad
lying forgotten in the fridge drawer,
or the fizzy drinks or milk
that no one would be drinking now,
perhaps tinned peas,
a tub of moldy cream cheese,
cubes of beef stock,
products past their sell-by dates

or bought recently (so much waste!)
at the local supermarket.
That's assuming the basics were there,
these days when
no one has any money
or work.
What we know is that he took the shelves
out of the fridge,
the high ones and the lower,
in order to fit in there
(in the section meant for Tupperware—
alongside leftovers—
and chilled water,
and cooked rice,
and pickled cucumbers)
the body of his wife,
Engel Sofia Pironato, 21 years old,
who he was separating from,
and whom he had strangled
with a well-administered chokehold
following a heated argument
that Monday morning.
After putting
his dead wife
in the fridge,
he spent the day
walking around the city,
troubled,

uncertain as to whether he should or should not
run away to his uncle's place
in Ermelino Matarazzo.

R

"IT'S ALL KICKING OFF RIGHT NOW!" bawled the radio presenter. "The temperature's mounting. Today's highlights, my boy: A man suffers an attempted murder in Jequetiba. Shots were fired!" The taxi driver was listening carefully.

"They don't say the victim's name, do they?" he complained. "They probably don't even know it. So many people are dying. Quite the slaughterhouse round here, hmm? They kill one, hang another, and on it goes."

Every time I was driven somewhere, I noticed the number of boarded-up houses in the city—and in the midst of the forest. The numbers of starving street dogs, the gaping garbage bins teeming with vultures, and the tarmac, riddled with potholes.

"There's the police station," he said, pointing out a cuboid building; one side had been painted sea-green.

The summons had reached me two days before—less than a week after Txupira's killers' deaths. With the letter in my handbag, I went in and identified myself.

The interrogation was over sooner than I'd expected. The officer thought I was a journalist, not a lawyer, and that I was in Cruzeiro do Sul to write about Txupira's death, not to attend hearings for cases of violence against women. He had trouble understanding that part. What were my aims in doing this? Why wasn't I doing my "monitoring" in São Paulo? And why was I still here in the city if the task force's formal campaign had come to an end? "I'm taking a sabbatical," I answered. Then I had to explain what a sabbatical is.

"Do you have some information that might help the investigation of the boys' case?"

It was frightening to see the rapid pace of the investigations into the deaths of the three boys. Rita's case was progressing at an altogether different tempo. In Brazil, the time required for justice is generally similar to that of Penelope's weaving. Not to mention the extra time required for documents to sit around in in-trays or for the systems to snarl in bureaucratic mumbo-jumbo. Yet the situation was quite different for Acre's founding fathers. The same dedication they'd applied to putting the brakes on Txupira's case, using every kind of delaying factor, was now put in service of pursuing the boys' case at first-world velocity.

I told Carla about it on Saturday, when she came to have lunch at my house. Marcos was preparing a tambaqui in the kitchen. After dressing the salad and setting the table, the two of us took our glasses of white wine to the veranda.

"There's something about this story that doesn't add up," Carla said. "There is an explanation for Txupira's murder. And I have a theory about Rita's death: she got too closely involved in investigating Txupira's case. But how do the three boys fit?"

"Couldn't it have been an isolated act of retribution by some Kuratawa villager?" I asked. "Their revenge?"

"If it were a revenge move, the cacique would know about it. At this point, he would already have told me. You saw it with your own eyes: they're all terrified."

According to her, the boys' deaths pointed to some factor we had missed altogether.

"What do you suspect?" I asked.

"We have open borders. I've already heard stories of riverine communities being coerced into storing cocaine for drug traffickers. Usually the base comes from Peru; at this point, they have a system for disposing of it via the Juruá river, downstream as far as the falls at Breu river."

"I did mention this to you. The place where Txupira was last seen caught my attention."

"I've been thinking about that too."

Over lunch, Marcos said he thought Carla's idea made sense. "It's so easy to give in to temptation. You cross the border, buy the coke, cheap as bananas, and get back here without going through a single police checkpoint. That's why Acre is like this: a guy can be a bog-standard clerk in an office one day, and the next, he's running a bunch of spanking-new petrol stations. Where did he get the cash for it?"

After lunch, we went into town. Marcos had promised to pick up some provisions for Zapira's village, and we took advantage of his journey to get a graviola ice cream in the central square.

We sat in silence, enjoying our ice creams, watching people coming and going amid the dozens of tacky shops selling every kind of trinket imaginable and the mayhem of children playing on the synthetic grass while their parents ate mixed grills or cassava kibbeh in the cafes around them, when suddenly Paulo growled by on his scooter. Seeing us, he stopped and came to join us. The atmosphere between him and Carla was decidedly tense. Rolling her eyes, practically hostile, with a fake smile on her face, Carla made it amply clear that his presence was unwanted. I felt sorry for the guy.

"Don't get too upset," she said, when we were alone again. Paulo had come to her house the night before when Denis was there, she told me. "I explained that we were working on Rita's case."

"Did he believe you?"

"That's his problem. I'm a grown-up, I've been around the block more than once, I pay my bills, I don't owe explanations to anyone. Besides, I already told him I wanted some time to myself, to concentrate on my work."

"Wouldn't it be easier if you told him the relationship's over? Just say it really clearly and simply?"

"I could hardly be clearer or more categorical, though I guess I haven't made him a comic strip version yet."

I had planned to go with Marcos to bring the groceries to Zapira's village, and persuaded Carla to come with us. I could almost have predicted what happened next. On the way, she said she'd like to try the ayahuasca tea. It was the first time she had shown any interest in the ritual, although we'd talked a lot about it.

I'd been running a low fever over the previous few days, generally worsening at the end of the day, so I decided not to take the tea this time. To my surprise, Zapira said I could help her guide the others. I already felt completely at ease among these people. Now, I saw with pleasure, I was being welcomed—no longer viewed as a tourist, a nosey outsider, or a sociologist gathering material. Considering the wary ethos of the community, this felt like no small achievement.

"What should I do?" I asked Zapira.

"Look after your friend," she replied.

When we stepped inside the maloca where the ritual was held, we found a large number of people from the city and a few foreigners already sitting on the mats laid out on the floor. We settled on the outer edge of the circle, where a sweet breeze wafted forest scents into the room.

Zapira came in, now wearing a kind of cotton smock, edged with açaí and pitomba seeds. On her head was a diadem decorated with toucan feathers; several necklaces of beads, birds' claws, and monkey teeth hung around her neck. While she gave a speech welcoming the community, Marcos, his skin glowing with the colors of the urucum, was moving around the room carrying a roughly made wooden censer burning a lump of white pitch. Soon the resinous fragrance filled the air. The rhythmic sound of the shakers was blending with the whirring of crickets and cicadas.

By this time, I already knew that the ceremonial songs were about a celebration in the sky where our siblings and cousins, aunts, uncles, parents, and all our dead relatives would be drinking ayahuasca tea and dancing around us. I noticed how the dancing, the beat, and the singing moved Carla, and considered how odd it was that she'd lived here for four years and, thanks to her role, was more accustomed to seeing the poverty of the indigenous people around us than their attempts to rebuild their identity.

Zapira gave her a dose of the brew.

After a long moment of dark, uneasy silence, Carla said only: "Sis, I feel bad."

When I took her outside to the clearing to get some air, I realized that I was feverish again. Carla vomited three times. Graviola ice cream. I gave her sips of water and wrapped her in my shawl. Then I gave her a few goji berries that I'd brought in my rucksack, to remedy the sour taste in her mouth.

A cool wind was blowing in the crowns of the trees around us.

"Breathe," I said, "and keep your eyes open."

We stayed out there a long while, silently holding hands, listening to the songs rising from the maloca and mingling with the sounds of the wind whipping up the river.

"Shall we go back in?" I asked, as she seemed to be feeling better.

We followed the beaten-earth path back, and she thanked me in good Acrean style: "Thanks, little sis."

I said I thought all the "lil bros" and "lil sis's" used so affectionately here were charming and poetic.

"It's different with you," she said. "You are the sister Acre has brought me."

A great wave of affection for her overtook me. Marcos joined us, and we sat together, huddled on the steps like a family, I thought, as I wrapped my shawl around the three of us, my two friends in their 'huasca trips and me sunk into a febrile torpor, moving in and out of a hollow, dreamless sleep.

The next day, we woke in cotton hammocks in the visitors' tepee and went to dip our toes in the village creek. I asked Carla about her experience the night before.

"My dreams were all about Rita," she said—and that reminded me of what Zapira had told me: that the tea could allow us to speak with the dead. I thought of the women who had appeared during my sessions, materializing in ghostly forms yet wearing bright colors, such reds, yellows, and blacks, some rising out of lakes, others dropping from the skies, some with roots for feet, others with bloodshot eyes or the bodies of jaguars, still others bringing me their prey and taking me to hunt with them, whispering secrets into my ears. What for me had always felt like an otherworldly revelation for Carla became a mirror to the real world. Rita falling down the stairs—Rita being thrown down the stairs—Rita laid out in the morgue—the Rita-doll in Serrano's tests. Rita in her coffin.

"Was that all?" I asked, thinking it was a shame, at least on the aesthetic front, that her Rita visions could not fly or speak flowers or roar secrets.

Carla said then that she could not digest Rita's death. Even if it had been an accident, which she refused to believe, "it was still a horribly pointless death, and fundamentally unacceptable."

Perhaps Rita was the first great loss in Carla's life. Perhaps Carla was overwhelmed by the revelation that what we call life is equally a queue for death. There are some, like my grandmother, who learn this—and learning it isn't the same as knowing it— and can never again look at the world without seeing death's shadow. It surprised me that Carla had come to the heart of the living forest and returned in the same shape in which she had entered it, untouched by any sense of mystery or awe. No pulsing colors in her visions, no flying jaguars or green stones; no giant cocks on allegorical floats; no Amazon women or glorious vengeances or marine waterfalls, filled with multicolored fish swimming around our Lady of the Green Stones' head. All Carla saw was this: a dream grounded in logic, with real-life visions. An enhancement of her natural faculties.

"In my dream, Rita's nails were painted red on the day she died," Carla said. "I want to check this with Serrano. It's an important detail, especially if she fought for her life. We should have found scraps of the polish on the stairs, don't you think?"

I could not help asking: "Why did you want to drink the ayahuasca?"

"You think because I'm an atheist I can't go into a cathedral and admire its beauty?" she replied.

I was properly ill for the rest of the day. Marcos told me that Zapira made me drink a tea of watercress, caper-plant, and chicory, to fend off the chill. But all I remember is being stuck on the BR-364 highway for a very long time, blocked by indigenous people protesting against yet another state-sanctioned kick in the teeth.

I only managed to try speaking to Carla again on Monday, after hearing on the radio, while having breakfast with Marcos, that a fire had broken out, and been subdued, in the Kuratawa's village. I called Carla's cell phone but didn't get through.

Next, I was surprised to learn that Carla hadn't shown up at the courthouse, even though her name was down for several hearings.

Marcos suggested we drop by her house. On the way, I called her phone again—still no answer. Then I called Denis, who was in Rio Branco. "I've not spoken to her since Saturday," he said. Paulo too had no news of her.

"The last time I saw you was in the square and you were with her," he said. "Why do you ask?"

By eleven that morning, Marcos and I were ringing Carla's doorbell. Nothing. Walking around the house, we saw that the back door was unlocked. I went in and called her name.

We found Carla lying facedown near the television in a pool of blood. Marcos picked up her wrist and looked at me in a way I'll never forget. I began to scream, a sharp, dry, piercing scream, a knife of a scream, a razor-blade, a dagger, filed thin, to bury deep in my own flesh.

12

THE SIMPLE ART OF KILLING A WOMAN, PART 2

Top of my pile
of dead women,
on a level with her right hypochondrium,
or more specifically halfway
between the right nipple and the belly button,
on the body of Carla Penteado, 40
(independent, highly experienced, and used to running her
own life),
an oval wound was identified,
smooth,
with even,
inverted,
reddish edges,
produced by the passage of the projectile
from a firearm.
Upon analysis of said projectile
by Acreano forensics
it was concluded that the foregoing object

was fired
from the same firearm
that killed
Crisântemo
& Abelardo
& Francisco.

S

"YELLOW IN THE MORNING, red in the afternoon, and blue at night," the nurse had explained when I woke up in the health center, some days earlier. The pills came in little colored baggies to make treatment of the indigenous and riverine peoples' malarial bouts easier. But I was the patient this time.

I couldn't remember how I'd reached the Ch'aska community, nor could I recall my first fit in front of the police officer. But I did remember the police coming to Carla's house, and her body being carried off to the morgue. A soundless memory, as if in a silent film. As if I hadn't been there, in the midst of that horror. I also remembered briefly waking at some point with an IV drip running into my arm. And the nurse explaining how I was to take the colored pills.

Marcos had suggested we take a break from the city after we'd made our statements to the police. I needed good treatment and rest. Besides—and unlike the police—he was aware of the risk I was running. They'd killed Rita, and now they'd murdered Carla, so what guarantee was there of my safety?

Now prostrate in my hammock inside the maloca, my body

was a diffuse mass of throbbing pain. The macaws' screeches in the clearing. Thunderclaps. Footsteps around me. The slightest sound hurt. The morning light seemed to tear craters in my retina. Any kind of smell made me nauseous. And now I was abruptly sucked into a polar vortex, swept up into a frozen knot, and my whole body was racked with uncontrollable spasms.

Soon enough, I learned that what I was experiencing was a kind of sensory overload, as if every aspect of reality were harsh, sharp, and excessively bright—these sensations that made my skin tense up and my eyes water were in fact the warning signs of another seizure. At these moments, Zapira would wrap me in a rough woollen cloth, the same way some mothers swaddle their babies, so my legs and arms were immobilized.

After each attack, I was drenched in sweat and felt drained, dead tired. I only stopped vomiting when Zapira threw out my colored pills.

"I'm going to do this my way," she said.

From the viewpoint of mainstream medicine, I was suffering from malaria, but to Zapira and her people, my problem was principally spiritual: caused by sorcery, by enemy spirits that circulate at night and feed by siphoning off our souls.

"Open your mouth. Drink this."

Her orders, which didn't always succeed in dragging me from my state of mental confusion and physical prostration, were preceded by the powerful aroma of banana porridge, roast corn, herbal infusions, and boiled cassava.

Frogs. Grubs. Wasps. Shades. Zapira could see the malevolent beings trying to take hold of my spirit. So while I burned or shivered, she was grating seeds and cooking up nutshells and macerating leaves—and pouring it all down my throat. She sang and danced around me and blew snuff into my nostrils. Now and then she had my body rubbed down and warmed with aromatic oils. Other times I was cooled with compresses, or immersed in a roughly hewn wooden trough of water tempered with charred herbs. Three times a day, she forced me to drink a spoonful of extremely bitter syrup.

Holding out against state neglect, enduring illegal burnings and the clandestine loggers' and agribusiness lobbies' daily incursions upon these peoples of the jaguar, the frogs, the sun, the peach and buriti palm—so many of the Amazon's people have now spent centuries at risk of extinction. Yet it was rare for me to open my eyes and find nobody at my side. Every day, men would bring me fish and women would cook or prepare teas for me and watch over my tormented writhing. At some point, I woke with children roaming around my hammock like bright beetles or big blue butterflies. As for Zapira, it's hard to overstate how well she cared for me.

"Don't be afraid of anything," she would say when I opened my eyes.

It's possible that, one day, I may no longer remember that dense, rich smell of earth warmed by the sun after a torrential jungle downpour. But I will never forget the unity maintained by the Ch'aska people, a unity that could never fit with the logic of trample-slash-burn-rob-and-sell—the stamp of every colonized country—and is instead rooted in the pulse of jungle life, in the endless unfurling of the cycles of birth, flowering, and return to earth. This now appeared to me to be patently fundamental to any hope of human survival.

If I'd followed the conventional treatment prescribed by the hospital, my recovery would have been quicker. With Zapira's herbs, however, the side effects were much reduced.

Little by little, my attacks grew fewer and less intense. My toenails had grown long! Soon I was able to leave the hammock. On good days, I would sit with the women and watch them weave bedding and dividers out of patauá straw for new malocas. I would go with them to wash clothes in the river, and often sat out on the veranda to catch the mild morning sunlight or play with the children. I liked showing the children photos of my home in São Paulo and of my grandmother and my friends. We would go for short walks to collect açaí. Over this period, I learned my first phrase in Tsai: "Hi, how are you?"

Later, Zapira explained that actually what I'd learned meant "My fart can kill alligators."

One sunny day, I woke up free of pain. My body was no longer a stage for malarial mosquito mischief. I could breathe without effort. I could walk without panting or debilitating shivers. My thoughts were as clear as water.

When I emerged from the hut, the bright daylight did not blister my eyes. My temples weren't screaming. I stopped to eat a banana and observe the bustle around me. Men with machetes and clubs were beating *jagube* vines in preparation for making the sacred brew; women were washing *chacrona* leaves. Zapira was sitting before a vast cauldron placing layers of clean leaves between the crushed cipó vines, layer upon layer. More firewood. More cipó. Another layer of chacrona leaves. Stoke the fire. Jagube. The air was almost still; just the smoke and the crackling fire. The women washing leaves, the men threshing out the vines—*pah, pah, pah*—and suddenly my heart and the machetes were beating to the same rhythm. Death has been kind to me, I thought. I haven't been run over by a lorry. I haven't fallen to a stray bullet. I have not been hastened toward death—rather, death has only dreamed of me; it has only knocked at my door. *Tap, tap, tap.* "I'm thinking of coming for you today at nightfall," death had said. Carla was not so lucky.

"She isn't here," I said aloud, as if to try out this truth.

Death plays a bluffing game with some people. With others, there's no discussion. I was here, thrumming with life, as alive as the men holding the machetes. I had withstood death; I had slammed the door in his face. "Wrong visitor," I told him, like in the Langston Hughes poem. I was here, and my heart was dancing to the machetes' music. But Carla was dead and Rita was dead. My mother was dead. Mountains of dead women stretched all around me—too many names recorded in my notebook. All those wasted lives. But I was alive. And I felt, I saw, the joy of living right before my eyes. Flights of parakeets, encircled by local people. The river right there. The forest here. I cried. To be here, alive, I felt as though I'd managed to go and take photos of the great black hole—and returned. I said hi to death, almost giggling with the thought—I'm alive. Heart and knives dancing to the same tune.

Then a gaggle of children surrounded me, nimble as birds, their hair wet from bathing in the river, and began shouting and pulling me along. They took me to the creek to show me Marcos drawing close in a motorized aluminum canoe.

Thanks to his classes at the university, Marcos tended to be free only on the weekends. So it was disconcerting to see him here on a Wednesday morning.

"They've caught the murderer," he said, as we both stepped inside the maloca where I was staying.

"Carla's murderer?"

"Carla's—and Crisântemo, Abelardo, and Francisco's."

"So it's the same person?"

"It's Gerson Pimentel."

He took the day's paper from his backpack. I looked at the murderer's mugshot: light eyes, moustache, slightly receding at the corners of a broad forehead.

Marcos asked if I knew him, and if I'd ever seen Carla with him.

"No. And I never even heard Carla mention his name."

"I thought it might be someone she helped to convict. But it says here he has no previous criminal record."

This didn't make sense. Pimentel might have killed the three boys, or he might have been Carla's killer—either was possible. But the notion of this one person being responsible for all four murders seemed absurd.

The article said that the killer was the manager of a cell phone shop and had been arrested for drunk-driving during a police raid. In his glove box, the police had found a .45 gun, a special commemorative Polten from 1911.

By coincidence, the officer who'd arrested Pimentel was a brother-in-law of the investigator who had been working on the boys' and Carla's cases, and he knew that the cartridges found at both crime scenes originated from a rare firearm.

On learning of the arrest, the investigator had sent the gun to forensics. Their report concluded that Pimentel's weapon was indeed the source of the bullets that had killed Carla and the three boys.

I couldn't make sense of it. "But what's his motive? Why would he commit these crimes?"

"Sick in the head. Crazy? No idea."

"No. This doesn't add up. It's a hell of a coincidence."

"Second possibility: he could have been hired by someone. A professional killer."

"Without any criminal record? Registered taxpayer and everything?"

I remembered our chat about drug trafficking in the region.

"We need to speak to Serrano," I said.

"I'll call him when we're back in Cruzeiro."

"Now," I said, picking up my bag. "We need to speak to him right now."

Two hours' boat ride and we would be in Mâncio Lima, where our phones could pick up a signal.

"Don't go now," Zapira pleaded, when I said goodbye. "You're still not well enough."

Marcos too was against my going. "A relapse can be worse than the original illness," he warned.

I kept my phone in my hand all the way back, monitoring

the signal. I called Serrano before even stepping out of the motorboat.

"Didn't you hear?" he asked. "Paulo's just turned himself in."

"Who?"

"Paulo. The boy Carla was seeing. He's wall-to-wall on television right now. He's the one who killed Carla and the other three."

We ran to a shop near the marina where a television sat perched on a stack of tiles, between a heap of bananas and another of garlic. No one was watching the *telenovela* that was playing.

I asked if we could change the channel, and there on the TV were the images of Crisântemo, Abelardo, and Francisco at the university campus, in their classrooms. "Crime solved," ran along the bar beneath the scenes. The presenter was saying that Paulo Alves was Gerson Pimentel's cousin and had stolen his gun in order to commit the murders. Upon learning of his cousin's arrest, Paulo had realized that Gerson should not be held responsible for his own crimes and decided to give himself up. "The police still don't know what motivated the killings," the journalist added.

Crisântemo's father was being mobbed by reporters outside the police station. "I promised my son I would not rest while his murderer was still at large," he said. "Now we'll find out the whole truth. We will have justice: that I guarantee."

There was only the smallest mention of Carla's death. In the photo used for the broadcast, she was wearing a bikini and relaxing in the sun by the river. She was a second-class corpse, a supporting actor in their show.

"S'what you get for messing with the Devil . . . "—said a tipsy old man who was sitting by the door alongside others who'd gathered around the TV as soon as we changed the channel. "You can bet on it," he said; "that lady was doing all four of them. There's pussy at the bottom of this, no doubt."

ETA

Flap, flap, flap. The pussies were gliding high above like the great flights of birds that heralded summer. Macaw-pussies, Swainson's hawk-pussies, slate-colored grosbeak-pussies. Flycatcher-pussies, pariri-pussies, and blue-crowned trogon-pussies. Sulphur-bellied neopelma-pussies, speckle-breasted antpitta-pussies, crested eagle-pussies, and cacique-pussies. There were so many of them and so brightly colored, some leading wide arrow formations, others flying alone, gliding solo in the blue sky.

And the women too kept on coming, some flying, some swimming, some on horseback, others skating. I came slowly, on foot, taking care where I stepped, now over fire, now ice, now over stretches of water. Some of the women were naked. Others wore a black redaction strip like a chastity belt. As fast as the redacted women could line up around the lake, so their pussies were reunited with them, flying back to their bodies. *Flap, flap, click.* I mean, our pussies simply fit back on with an automatic click, freeing us of our black strips.

From among the women, Txupira spoke up. It was different for her, she said. Her pussy would not fly back to her as the others were doing. Hours earlier, she had found her genitals tossed onto a heap labelled "pink pussies."

"For sale?" one warrior asked.

The tallest one nodded. "In the market for pussies, the pink ones sell for the highest prices."

"That's why we're getting operations on our vaginas," said another. The others began to chime in.

"They cut back the outer lips."

"They reduce our Mons Venus."

"And tighten up our tubes."

"And whiten our cunts."

All of them together: "The butchers! The slaughterers!"

I said: "They hunt our pussies with nets, as if we were butterflies."

Txupira: "Nothing bothers them quite as much as an independent pussy!"

"They say a pussy in the hand is worth two in flight."

Carla, who had joined us without my noticing, said: "Hang on till we know what's best to do with these collectors of pink pussies."

"Kill the bastards," one woman said.

"They were pedophiles."

"Pedophiles like pink pussies."

"The pedophile wolf-whistled when Txupira got her vagina back. 'What a fine vagina,' he said, before they lynched him."

At this point we were all in possession of our pussies, happily gathered around the lake, laughing together and waiting for the big moment.

"Is she really coming?" Carla asked.

All at once, the whole lake began to glow, illuminating not only the Lady of the Green Stones rising up through it but also a retinue of young indigenous children. Hundreds of fish of all colors glimmered upon her vestments.

We sang and danced in her honor.

Carê pari— Take your stone, we sang.

Catê pari— Sing your stone.

Domi pari— Look to your stone, we commanded.

I looked down at the green stone in my hands. In it I could see the mysterious key symbol, *ting, ting, ting*, and I'm here, again, I'm a child, I stare at the key shining in the ignition of a car that isn't my mother's or my father's, the keys glint and jangle, *ting, ting*, and I'm afraid and alone in the back seat, the radio is playing the song *Ob-la-di ob-la-da life goes on bra* . . . and before I woke up here, in this steep canyon, I woke up in my new bed with the mermaid bedspread, in my dad's new house; I woke to my mother's voice. "Stop it," she was saying, "stop doing this," and I walked barefoot out into the hall and she's here, my mother, beautiful in her black dress with the white spots, she's here to fetch me. "Hello, my darling, shall we go home?" she asks. "Go to your room," my father says, shouting, "Straight to your room," he says again. I look at my beautiful, terrified mother, not knowing this is the last time I will see her, and in bed I listen to her sobs. "Enough," she says, "It's over," she says, "Let me go," she says, I cry, I sob, I cover my ears, "Don't do this," she says, I listen to her screams, her calls for help, and more screaming, and help, I burrow right under the sheets, shaking, weeping, and whispering, Mommy, very softly, Mommy, Mommy, Mommy, Mommy, then suddenly silence. Silence, silence, silence, and more silence. A sea of silence. A sharp silence, frozen silence, dangerous silence. When I finally gather the courage and come out from under my sheets, and leave my room, I find my father on all fours, scrubbing the living room floor. *Shp, shp, shp*. The cleaning cloth in his hands absorbs the red liquid which is spread over the floor and spattered inside the bucket, where the water is turning as red as Mommy's nail polish. "Did you wake up, my princess? Let's go to your room so I can tuck you in."

And when I wake again, in the back of that unfamiliar car, *Ob-la-di ob-la-da*, it's dark outside. I stand up on the seat. Then I see that my mother's car is directly in front, lit by the headlights of the one I am in. With the help of a strong man wearing a cap, my father is taking a bundle wrapped in my mermaid bedspread out of the boot, and the mermaid's tail now has a big red patch on it. The pair of them slide the bundle into the driver's seat of Mommy's car, then pull the bedcover off. And they shove her car until it rolls over into the canyon.

Now I wake up in my grandmother's lap. We are in the church. Close to us lies the coffin holding my mother's body, ringed with flowers.

"You know," Grandma says, "the constellations we can see in the skies are made of the people we love." And she tries to persuade me that my mother is a star now. "Let's go outside, I'll show you your mommy's star," she says, taking my hand.

And once more I wake up. *Ob-la-di ob-la-da*. The Lady of the Green Stones is beside me now, on the edge of the chasm. At the top. Hawks glide along the horizon. She is showing me my mother's car smashed below.

I launch myself over the cliff, horrified, my heart almost leaping from my mouth. But see now, as soon as I'm in the valley, there's no car here at all. Where the car was, there is a pile of dead women. Some in skirts, others naked, some headless, others shoeless, this one skinny, that one old, this one expensively dressed, that one sliced to pieces, this from Roraima, that from Fortaleza, and this one married, this one single, this from São Paulo, that from Ubatuba, this from the North, that from the South, this one a teacher, this a maid, that one almost white, this one Black, that one Black, the one there Black, and another, and this one too, one more Black woman and another, there are so many of them, of all

ages, but more young than old, more Black than white, and right
at the head of them all is Carla.

& Rita is just behind her.

& Engel is there too.

& Taita.

& Daniela.

& Lilian Maria.

& Scarlath.

& Alessandra.

& Rayane.

& Marciane.

& Tatiana.

& Queila.

& Fabíola.

& Degmar.

& Soraia.

& Jaqueline.

& Juciele.

& Almecina.

& Suzyane.

& Elaine.

& Fernanda.

& Iza.

& Ketlen.

& Raele.

& Eudinéia.

& Txupira.

The pile is endless.

The pile is monstrous.

The pile is outrageous.

Already I am in tears

when I see
buried
beneath the mountain of murdered
women:
my
mother.

And all I can see of her is one arm partly covered by the sleeve of her black dress with the white spots. The ring with the green gemstone, her red nails. The rest of her body is lost beneath the great mound of bodies.

I go to her. I take hold of my mother's hand and sit down. My mother and I, together. Me and all the dead women.

Once more, piercing metallic laughter, like knives being sharpened, rings and hisses in my ears.

And then, with a sudden effort, I put all my strength into dragging my mother out from beneath that great pile of women. In doing so, it seems, I undermine some logic, I undo an equilibrium, or more likely, I break some kind of spell—and all the women take off and fly away like a flock of the local thrushes, there are so many, they could be a flight of kingbirds, or flycatchers, or blue-winged teal, or jabiru stork and Pantanal snipe, or sandpipers, little cuckoos and variegated flycatchers; they fly up high, criss-cross the skies, chittering, some heading south, others to the north, only the two of us are here still, my mother and I, holding hands.

I can smell her mother's smell, her warmth.

She kisses my hand.

"How lovely!" she says, looking at my long fingers in surprise. "We have the same hands: the same proportions, the same shape nails."

I feel an energy flow into my body from hers and then return to hers and flow back into mine, a kind of joyous short-circuit, endless and loving.

Still holding hands, we walk to the lake where we can see ourselves reflected: she becomes me and I become her.

"Mother and daughter," she says, exulting.

Ob-la-di ob-la-da . . . that song starts up again.

She raises a finger: "Can you hear it?"

"It's coming from there," I say, pointing to her car, parked on the side of the road.

"Did Heaven descend or the Earth rise up?" my mother wonders. "It's scorching out!"

I suggest, with a thrill: "Shall we go for a swim?"

Flap, flap, flap. Our wings beat in time and we take flight.

T

EXHIBIT TO BE FILED under case number 001976-36-2014.
8.27.0082.

Press play on the video recording and you will see:

It's raining. A boat is moored at the border of the Kuratawa
territory. Balancing in it, a strong-looking, bare-chested man
takes something out of a basket at his feet and throws it to a
boy standing on the land nearby.

If you zoom in, you can see that the one on terra firma is
Crisântemo. He takes the brick-sized package, which is white
and wrapped in plastic, and passes it to a boy standing behind
him—Francisco, who, along with Abelardo, lays the package
in a shallow pit.

It's a poor-quality video. The first frames are taken from
some distance away, but the quality improves as the person
filming comes closer to the scene.

At one minute eight seconds in, it's clear that what we're
watching is the off-loading and secret storage of cocaine.

Now the camera is close to the action. We can clearly see the packets being stored in the hole.

Suddenly, something makes Francisco look up. He turns to the camera and points directly at it.

He says: "Hey, someone's there!"

Now we see a sequence of images like those captured by war reporters in conflict zones. Jungle, sky, ground, riverbanks, no focus or definition, juddering violently with the scramble to escape.

The audio is worth our attention too. Gasping breaths, hurried steps and voices.

Male voice: "There, over there!"

Running.

Another voice off: "That way, catch her! Get her!"

Another voice: "Don't let her go—catch her!"

Panicked breathing. A woman screams.

A voice: "Cool it, girl. Quiet!"

The girl: "No! No!"

Male voice: "Give me her phone."

And then we see Crisântemo appear, filling the screen. "The slut is recording us!"

And the camera is turned off.

The date of the recording is the same as that of Txupira's disappearance.

U

"AAAAAH. THAT *IS* LOVELY." Children calling. "Ooooh. Sooo nice." Dona Yolanda in fits of laughter. "How lovely, how cool!"

I woke to the unmistakable sound of my grandmother's voice emanating from the village clearing.

I leaped out of the hammock and ran to the window. On the far edge, Marcos and a few other grown-ups were playing football with a group of kids.

In the damp and steaming center of the clearing, Zapira was sitting with my grandmother below a cashew tree, the pair of them surrounded by girls. My heart filled with joy.

We embraced for a long time; we had missed each other—I complained she should have woken me, she that I needed my rest—and then we sat arm in arm at Zapira's side, watching the children play in the shade of the cashew. They were drawing seeds, frogs, toothy animal maws, pacas, and javalis in ballpoint pen on the faces of the dolls my grandma had brought from São Paulo as presents. Although visibly tired from her journey, my grandmother asked about the figures, so Zapira told us the origin myth of her people, the children of Takuna—a story I had heard many times.

Takuna was a solitary goddess who lived on the sun, in a cave beside which grew a *cuiatá* plant, a holy tree whose seeds ensured the goddess stayed healthy and beautiful. Although she was strong and healthy, Takuna was not happy. She could not play or debate or dance or sing because there was no one else up there in her cave on the sun. So Takuna went on moping until Sun had an idea. With every cuiatá bud she ate, the seed she spat out would lie in the sunlight and grow warm, and then it would sprout and transform into some other species: one into a cashew tree, another into a banana palm, this one into biribá and that into graviola, some as red as blood, others yellow as Sun, many of them green and a few brown, each tastier than the last. Soon there were so many new plants growing together that they no longer fit inside the cave, so Sun turned Takuna's cave inside-out—and a forest was born. Now Takuna was happy because she could walk through the forest and eat its brightly colored fruits, but when she realized that the plants wouldn't sing, she grew sad once more. *Aie, aie, aie,* she wept. To cheer the goddess, Sun began to grow some of his cuiatá seeds into songbirds. From one seed the black-capped Tinamou was born, from another came the sapphire-spangled Emerald, and now the semicollared puffbird, the fulvous-chinned nunlet, the black-capped parakeet and the bluish-slate antshrike, and he saw such joy in Takuna's eyes that Sun got quite carried away and went on creating more and more, and thus were born all the animals that live in our jungle: the sloth, the porpoise, the ant, the piranha, the manatee, the alligator, the wild parrot, electric eel, giant anteater, capybara, and painted jaguar. As not all the creatures could live in the jungle, Sun had to invent rivers. Takuna was filled with glee by such loveliness but finally, when she realized she had no one with whom to share the birds' beauty and the rivers' melodious flowing, nor the sounds of the creatures as they chirruped and lowed and howled and squawked and bleated and croaked and brayed and barked and growled, she grew despondent again. *Aie, aie, aie,* she lamented. Will nothing make Takuna happy? Sun wondered, now troubled by his melancholy goddess. I give her biribá sugar apples and wild parrots and fast-flowing rivers and alligators, and all she can do is grizzle? So he closed his eyes and the night was born. The jatobá cherries grew; the rubber trees matured; the palms doubled in size. The young plants grew to adulthood. But Takuna could not shake her funk: *Aie, aie aie!* Her weeping and lamenting went on so long that Sun felt sorry for her again. He licked away her tears, which soaked the forest floor; thus, with his sunny saliva and his rays of sunlight, combined with the forest humus and Takuna's tears, a brave and warlike god called Zimu grew. Takuna rapidly fell in love. From their union were born many children, some the color of rose apples, others honey-hued, some more chestnut, others almost tan, but all of their tones were borne up from the earth through the stems of these new beings: people of the forest. Takuna and Zimu's love was so strong and beautiful that together they shone brighter than the dawn. This Sun did not like, and from his envy of their love arose the wicked spirits and all the thunderbolts, bad spells, raiders, lightning strikes, the whites, the diseases, feuds, governments, loggers, weaknesses, gold miners, massacres, betrayals, illegal burnings, plagues, slights, and other bad things in the world.

In return for wishing to burn brighter than Sun, Takuna was turned into the moon.

From her seat in the sky, she watches over her children.

Perhaps fatigued by the long story, or because she didn't know my grandmother so well, Zapira left out the loveliest part of the story, which is that Sun gave every being he created its own personal, internal sun, an idea of the soul as aligned with knowledge, filling the heavens and the forest after we die.

When her tale was done, Zapira went back to showing us cuiatá seed patterns on the dolls' cheeks.

"It's protection," she said.

"What about Zimu?" my grandmother asked   she was used to endings more like those of her regular TV series.

"Zimu was turned into the painted jaguar who keeps watch over the forest."

"He didn't die?"

"Every cacique has some of Zimu's warrior spirit in him," Zapira replied.

And did Zimu's spirit ever return to be with Takuna—in the moon, perhaps? Did they stay in love? And what about the envious spirits? How should we protect ourselves from their spells? Does the sun still envy Takuna? And isn't the moon now angry with the sun?

Plunged deep into these stories ("It would make a wonderful miniseries, don't you think?"), my grandmother spent two days pestering Zapira with questions.

"Dona Yolanda doesn't pause for breath, does she," Zapira remarked, weary of finding answers. By the end of our stay, Grandma had only to approach with her endless stream of questions (What's this flower called? And this tree? And that one? What is this for? And that? . . .) for Zapira to vanish rapidly into the darkness of the maloca.

There was only one moment that silenced my grandmother: when Marcos and I took her into the forest. The rain had just stopped and it felt as if we might grasp pure oxygen with both hands. Above us, the tapestry of branches and leaves was so tightly woven, we could hardly see the morning light. My grandma squatted like an indigenous woman getting ready to give birth and stayed there, listening to the sounds of the forest, the water, and the birds. She told us the jungle reminded her of a cathedral.

"I'd say that, if an atheist were to experience this, even they might start believing in God," she said.

During the many weeks I had spent with the Ch'aska, I felt they were giving me more than I could give in return. When it was time to say goodbye, I wept like a child.

"You will come back," Zapira said, holding me tightly. "You are family."

My grandma stepped in to join our circle: "We will come back, my girl. We *are* family"—she said this more than once on seeing my sadness over the next few days.

I still had much to do in Cruzeiro do Sul before leaving. I talked to Lena about potentially leaving her dog Oto with Marcos. He adored the dog and had looked after him all the time I had stayed in the village.

Lena liked the idea. Her return to Cruzeiro was still two months away.

I paid the electricity and water bills and, along with Grandma and Marcos, tidied the back garden, clipping away the overgrown bush.

We packed our suitcases on Sunday night, then Marcos and I took my grandmother for a dinner of tambaqui in the city. It had been a long time since I'd seen Grandma as happy as she was during this week we spent together, despite suffering from the heat. Her favorite outing was the walk along the creeks, which we always did in the late afternoons, when the temperature began to drop. She also loved walking around the center of town, and had already bought five kilos of local flour to bring back for her friends.

That night, when we walked into the restaurant, I saw Denis sitting alone at a corner table. He looked even more depressed than when he'd come to see me in the hospital.

"I tried to call you yesterday," I said, as we greeted each other.

"Won't you join me?" he asked.

Before we'd even ordered, we were already talking about Carla.

Denis told us that, the night Paulo discovered him and Carla in her house, he picked up "something bad in Paulo's expression, a kind of toxic energy; I even asked Carla if she felt it, too."

"Things still don't add up for me," Marcos said. "I liked him."

"Serrano told me he read Paulo's statement," Denis said.

According to Serrano, Paulo's version was that he killed the three boys in order to protect Carla, that he feared her life was in danger from them.

Denis went on: "In his statement, Paulo attests that you and Carla were threatened by the three boys in a nightclub. Is that true?"

"Yes," I said. "Paulo was there and he helped us."

"The defense will want you to testify," said Denis.

"Tell them not to hold their breath," my grandmother shot back.

"Did anyone help him?" Marcos wanted to know. "I don't see how he could have overpowered three strong young men . . . "

"He went for Crisântemo first," Denis said. "Took him out to the Corixo highway, tied him up and made him call Abelardo, saying he had important information about Txupira's trial. Abelardo came to meet his friend and fell into the trap there. Then Paulo did the same with Francisco."

But Denis's next revelation was the most shocking. "I finally found what it was that Rita had wanted to show Carla," he said, and opened his phone to show us a photo of an old cell phone.

"This was Txupira's," he said. "It was in the pocket of one of my sister's coats, in the closet. I thought it was odd, not only that it was *there*, but also that it was such an old model and so covered in dirt. When I charged it up, I found lots of photos of the Kuratawa and of Txupira. Then, in the middle, I found this"—he tapped play on a video that showed Crisântemo, Abelardo, and Francisco stashing drugs in a place very close to where Txupira was last seen, where I had been with Naia all that while before. But the most valuable element was the recording of the exact moment when Txupira was captured by the boys, just before she was killed.

"This will be as critical at the trial as a confession from the defendants," I said.

"How could Rita have come by this phone?" Marcos asked.

"I don't know. Probably someone sent it to her anonymously."

"Someone who knew the murderers," my grandma said.

"I have a theory," Denis admitted. "I heard that Crisântemo's girlfriend, the one who gave a statement for the defense at his trial, recently broke up with him, then moved out of Acre. Now she's studying in Miami. What's strange is that she deleted all her social media accounts. Have you ever heard of that—a girl of twenty-two without any online life? And who drops out of college in the middle of a semester to move to Miami? My guess is Crisântemo had Txupira's phone. And his relationship ended when the girlfriend found the phone and realized the lover boy she'd defended in court was actually a murdering rapist. That's why she decided to send the phone to Rita, who'd been writing articles about the crime."

"It's a theory. What are you going to do with it?" I asked.

"I've already done it. I went to the police."

"And?"

"*Nada.*"

"What do you mean, *nada*?" I asked.

229

"They did nothing at all. According to what they told me, this evidence can only be presented at Txupira's inquiry. But now that its presumed creators, the defendants, are dead, that case is closed."

"You should put the video online," my grandma suggested.

"I think so too," Marcos agreed.

"At least then everyone will know exactly what happened to Txupira."

We sat there with our drinks, subdued.

Denis knew a move like that could bring a lot of unintended consequences. We all knew it.

"I have to think," he said.

Before we left, Denis told us that the investigation into Rita's death was almost at a standstill. They hadn't even scheduled a date for a review of the two conflicting autopsy reports filed by Serrano and the investigator who'd done the original report.

"This one's going to take the long route," he said, dejectedly. "We all know how justice proceeds in this country."

"I need another drink," my grandma said, after Denis left. "Something nice and sweet—right now!"

We were paying the bill a few minutes later when my phone rang. It was the officer in charge of the inquiry into Carla's murder. I had been to the police station to meet him on Thursday; now he had an answer to my question.

"You can come here tomorrow," he said. "Paulo has agreed to see you."

V

HELLO, KILLER! When Paulo came into the visitors' room with a relaxed smile on his face, I wanted to lob those words at him, turn around, and get straight out again.

A criminal lawyer quickly learns that every homicide has a sob story in their back pocket. And it's often much more than the routine walk-through required for their defense in a court of law. The classic scene you know from movies when the lawyer argues with their client after catching them lying is always more complicated in real life. Before lying to the police, their family, their lawyer, their priest, their jury, and to society, the murderer has generally lied to themselves. Despite their crime, they have to believe they're still human.

If I genuinely had no interest in anything Paulo might tell me, why on earth was I here? I'd wondered, as I made my way from the car beforehand. What had prompted me to ask permission from the head of the city jail and from the judge to visit this man who was now smiling and holding his hand out—as if we were friends?

"Marcos didn't want to come with you?" he asked.

"No," I replied.

He avoided meeting my eyes. Other prisoners around us were talking with family members or their lawyers. I sat and faced him. He kept shifting his legs.

"I'm properly fucked, right?" he asked.

Seeing him there in his gray sweatshirt and yellow flip-flops, I thought of my father. I'd received so many letters from him when he was in prison. "Dear Bunny-rabbit"—they all began like that. At first, my grandad used to read them to me, as Grandma refused point-blank to do it. But the dear bunny-rabbit never replied to any of them. I remember when I turned ten, my grandad told me that in spite of all the things Grandma used to say about my dad, I had the right to see him, and that if I wanted to, he could take me for a visit. But I never went. After my father was granted conditional release, we moved several times, to live in different towns. He always found us. After he died, I began to wonder whether, if I had answered his letters, if I had visited him, I would have come to understand why he did what he did. And yet, sitting there before Paulo, I suddenly realized that understanding it wouldn't have fixed fuck-all. Even if my father had told me everything. Even if Paulo didn't lie. Even if I could get inside both their heads and see all the emotional shit they each had in there; even if I could know about all their traumas, their abandonments, their weaknesses; if I could do a full autopsy on both their psyches, isolate their fucked-up or sick or prejudiced minds in test tubes and see with my own eyes where that will to press the trigger came from, to blow off this woman's head or throttle that one, to cut short the lives of both so brutally; even so, my mother's death and Carla's death and the deaths of all those women filling my notebook would continue to make no sense at all.

"She was having an affair with Denis—did you know?"

I didn't reply.

"I'm starting to hate you as well," he said. "You don't know anything, isn't that right?"

I stood and waved to a guard.

"Sorry," he said, getting up too. "Please. Sit down. We need to talk. I always liked you. You always respected me. We got on. Shall we try to hold on to that—the respect?"

I took the pack of cigarettes from my bag and offered him one. We sat down again, facing each other.

"Thanks," he said, lighting the cigarette. "When I found out you'd asked to visit, I said to myself: Shit, she's actually reading my mind"—and with a thoughtful expression, he blew the smoke away to the side.

Then he told me he had no money for a lawyer. Each of his statements was bookended by long pauses, as if he were testing me.

"They've given me a really weak guy from the state legal office," he said. "He's done nothing so far. Nothing. Hasn't helped with anything. I thought you might be able to defend my case."

"Really?"

"In a way you owe it to me," he said.

"I owe you?"

"That night, in the club, you saw with your own eyes," he said. "You saw what happens to people like you and Carla, who come here knowing nothing about the city, getting in with the big guns, waking a few snakes. There's one crucial detail you forget when you come here: Acre is not São Paulo. We have our own ways of solving problems here."

"What I do know," I replied, "is that, if the Public Defender's Office makes any effort over your case, it won't be because they care a jot about Carla's death but because you also killed the city's three crown princes."

"Sure. But all the mistakes I've made were attempts to protect her—to protect Carla, your friend. And you. You also benefited from my mistakes; don't think I didn't see. You saw what happened to Txupira. You didn't know, but three months ago, a friend of my dad's gave me a job as a bouncer at a gun club. You can't imagine the things I heard in that place. They were going to do to Carla what they already did to Txupira. They also had their sights on you. You know, these are the guys who run the show. Perhaps you can't see it, but Acre has its rulers. You don't know how many Txupiras have already died—nobody knows. No one's in prison. Nothing happens. As for the Crisântemos round here, they simply won't accept that some misguided Carla full of her own theories, a city slicker without a clue, can suddenly show up here and think she can point her finger at the big men's dirty business. That's not how things work here in Acre."

He lowered his voice to tell me he would never let his cousin carry the can for him again.

"I have principles," he said. "I stand up for what I believe in."

Paulo had no trouble accepting his responsibility for the three boys' deaths. Perhaps because, as he expressed it, "Those guys were the worst kind of people. Little rich kids with no empathy for those around them. Arrogant people, the kind who've never wanted for anything. Besides, they were rapists. The whole city knows it. And here in Acre, we don't like rapists. So they have money, so they're important, that doesn't change the fact they're rapists. And in this part of the world, we don't like that. You know how rapists work: today they rape an Indian girl, tomorrow it's your sister. You know, there's a high chance we'll persuade the jury. That's why I'm confident. Really. The city will be on my side. Whether it's tomorrow or any day, nobody wants their sister raped. Everyone will understand I was only protecting Carla."

Paulo told his story as if Carla were still alive. I don't know if he had any idea how irrational he sounded. Perhaps he took my silence for assent. Or perhaps he actually believed what he was saying.

"I have photos on my phone," he continued. "Photos of those pieces of shit hanging around the courthouse, lying in wait for Carla. And I've got photos of the three of them near Carla's house. And in the club that night, closing in on you two. I have proof. I can explain myself. Don't imagine I'm some idiot who acted without thinking."

Up to that point, although it wasn't easy, I could still see vestiges of the kid who'd been Carla's boyfriend, the guy who used to come out with us now and then. But then Paulo delivered the final twist to his tale and laid the blame for his crime on Carla. His eyes gained a new gleam. Killing Carla was his life's great project, I thought.

"The problem is, I did all that stuff trying to protect the wrong person, you see? I fucked myself. Because while I was worried about Carla's safety, her well-being, her so snowed-under with work because of the dead Indian girl, and thanks to Rita poking her nose where she shouldn't, while I was getting my head in a twist trying to catch those rich-boy rapists, what was she up to? She was fucking Denis."

Occasionally, he would stop speaking and make a long pause, perhaps hoping I would say something. But I couldn't open my mouth.

"I asked her a hundred times if she was seeing Denis," Paulo said. "You know, everyone has a limit. My patience isn't endless. That Saturday, I went to Carla's house to say precisely that. I was very clear, I said: 'Carla, everyone has their limit.' I said she didn't know how to appreciate the people who really cared for her. I said, 'You don't appreciate the people who deserve it.' I said, 'I'm the one who's looking after you.' And her pretending this was all news to her, you know? She kept asking, 'What? What d'you mean?' I said, 'You think you can come here to Cruzeiro and hang out with those guys who have money to burn, let your hair down, and there won't be any consequences? Where do you think you are? You should be thanking me for getting those three rapists off your back. Don't pretend it was Denis who sorted them out for you.' That was when I realized that, despite everything, she was ungrateful. She kept saying, 'What are you talking about?' like some stupid parrot. 'What are you talking about?' Shit. Dammit! She made me so angry. I showed her the photos of Crisântemo, Abelardo, and Francisco staking out the courthouse and the ones of them skulking around her house. You know what she did then? Accused me of stalking her. Following her around. Isn't that fucked up? How could she be so clueless? I said: 'Girl, they were out to get you! Everything I've done has been to protect you! If it weren't for me, right now you'd be six feet under.' Then she said: 'What's all this crap about, if-not-for-me?' So I said: 'Don't you think Txupira's murderers, who were giving your whole team gray hair, you don't believe they were killed by some random cowboy out there, do you? Because if that's what you think, then you're a stubborn stupid slut.' 'Who are you talking about?'—she kept on asking me that. Such a fury she got me in. The way she was looking at me. You know, like she was, I dunno, the queen of the whole country? Lady Muck. As if I was, I dunno, an object you just use and then throw out? She was talking a heap of shit. So I showed her the revolver I'd been using to protect her. I know that was a mistake. The gun really made her flip. She started screaming, out of control, like she was really crazy. That was very bad. From there on, everything was fucked. I lost control. She was screaming and I just couldn't think straight. I said, 'Shut your mouth, Carla, stop being hysterical.' She wouldn't listen. She just kept screaming and screaming. When I tried to get a bit closer, she pushed me away—she gave me a slap and called me a bum, a waste of space. I'm being very open with you. You have to tell your lawyer the whole truth, I know that. She called me a layabout. She was giving me so much shit. It was crazy. I was keeping my cool. But when she got her phone and said she was going to call the police on me, I couldn't take it anymore."

Now he was weeping.

"Carla's problem," he said then, wiping his eyes with the edge of his shirt, "was she wouldn't let anyone help her. That was her problem."

His own error, he concluded, was having brought his gun with him to Carla's house.

"I don't know what happened to us. Everything was great between us. I don't know. Then everything went bad, from one minute to the next. At first I thought it was because of Txupira. We started to go wrong when Txupira's case opened. Before that murder, Carla was an ordinary person, working as usual. But Txupira's death changed everything. And then when Rita died, it got even worse. It messed up her head, you know? And suddenly our lives went to shit."

We sat there in silence for a few minutes.

"What now?" he finally managed to ask.

It's fascinating how rapidly silence can break a person down at a moment like this.

"Don't you have any ideas?" he asked, after a time.

"About what?"

"Defending me!"

"I suggest you ask that of your lawyer."

"You can't take my case?"

"No."

"What? I can't count on you?"

"No," I replied, getting to my feet.

"Hang on. Really? You're not going to defend me?"

"No."

He sat there looking at me while I gave the sign for a guard to step in.

"Can you tell me why?"

"No," I said, beginning to walk away.

"Why did you come here then?" he called, but I was already leaving the room.

I had no answer to give him. Hearing the click of the door closing behind me, I hastened my step, following the officer with a sense of urgency. I didn't want to be held up. My grandmother was waiting at the best ice cream parlor in Cruzeiro do Sul.

W

ATTENTION PASSENGERS *for flight RX 4679 to destination São Paulo. Could you please make your way to gate number 2.*

My eyes lit directly on the *Diário da Estrela*'s headline, where it lay on the newsstand: "Snow Boys." The title was a direct reference to the headline in another paper, one with connections in the local oligarchy, which had appeared on the occasion of Txupira's murderers' funeral: "Golden Boys." The photo illustrating today's article was a still from the video on Txupira's phone. It showed Crisântemo, Abelardo, and Francisco burying packets of cocaine on the Kuratawa land.

Hats off, Denis. According to the article, the night before, he had gone to the paper where his sister had worked until her death and told the editors the story I'd already heard.

The staggering thing about his story was that, even after receiving the video with the incriminating scenes, Cruzeiro's police had not initiated an investigation to see if there were any drugs hidden on the Kuratawa territory, nor to identify the kid in the boat who'd been helping the trio. "Our team is stretched too thin," explained the policeman in the article. "We continue to implement a range of measures in order to determine the accuracy of these claims."

My grandmother had already checked us in and was now waving to me from the flight desk, indicating I should get a move on. It was very early in the day to be calling Denis but I wanted to call now.

"You're leaving at the right time," he remarked, his voice still thick with sleep.

"Take care," I said. "You've made some powerful enemies."

Denis promised he would keep me abreast of the investigation into Rita's death and of Paulo's trial.

We took our seats in good time. It was Wednesday, and a public holiday—perhaps that was why our plane had so few passengers.

When Grandma got to the end of the article, we had already taken off.

"If I were you," she said, "I would steer clear of Acre for a while. At least until this case cools off."

"Aren't you sleepy?" I asked.

"Not after reading this," she replied, slipping the paper into the pocket of the seat in front of her.

"I want to tell you about something important that happened to me here," I said.

She looked at me anxiously.

"Something bad?"

"I remembered everything," I said.

"About what?"

"The night my mother was killed."

We sat in silence for a few moments. She gripped my hand tightly. And then, with a composure that surprised us both, I began to speak. First I explained what ayahuasca is, and about its capacity to activate the part of our brains that stores emotional memory, according to recent scientific research I had been reading. Then I described our sessions with the ayahuasca tea at Zapira's village. I described my visions, from the initial image of the key engraved on a green stone, to the whole puzzle of that night and its gradual coming together piece by piece: my mother arriving at my father's new house to fetch me, her black polka-dot dress, her ring with the green gemstone, my father sending me to my room, my mermaid bedspread, their fight, my father cleaning up the blood on the living room floor, the mermaid bedspread used to wrap my mother's body, the Beatles tune playing on the car radio, my waking up on the highway in a strange car, my father and a man I didn't know pushing my mother's car off a cliff's edge.

More than once, my grandmother's eyes filled with tears. She listened without interrupting.

I knew just how devastating all this was for her. Up to this point, we had not talked so openly about what happened. We had talked about my mother's absence, about missing her, about things we'd done together. But about the crime itself—never. Never about *how* my father had killed my mother. We had never spoken the word "murder." Perhaps that was my fault. Perhaps, if I'd asked earlier, my grandmother would have told me the truth about the investigation into my mother's murder. Perhaps my memories could have been recovered earlier, even without the ayahuasca's help. But the truth is, I'd never wanted to talk about it. Grown up and studying law at university, I hadn't even wanted to read about my mother's death.

"Please," I said now. "Please tell me what I don't know."

So she told me.

"It was a Sunday. You were spending the weekend on the little farm your father had rented, after the separation, not far from Monteiro Lobato, a town on the old highway to Campos de Jordão. He'd promised to bring you back to our house at the end of the day, but around three that afternoon, he called your mother to say he was only coming back to São Paulo on the Monday or Tuesday because his car had a problem that needed fixing before the journey. Your mother didn't like this; she suspected your father had some plan to try to keep you, and that's why she came to collect you from the farm.

"Around nine that night, he called me to ask if I knew where she was. I was surprised she wasn't there already. I tried to call your mother but the call wouldn't go through. Your grandfather and I were already very worried when, two hours later, we received a call from the police in Monteiro Lobato. Your mother had had an accident on the highway.

"Right away, I called your father. Until this point, I have to say, I liked him. Only some time after your mother died, during the inquiry into her death, in fact, did I discover how abusive he was toward her. Your mother never said anything about that. Even when they were separating, she didn't say. Your father was a clever man, and good company; no one could have imagined he was abusing your mother, never mind that he might even be plotting to kill her. He still occasionally came to our house to ask for help or advice; he really hadn't wanted the separation to happen at all. So that night, after I called him, your grandad and I went to Monteiro Lobato. Your father drove in a friend's car to meet us at the site of the accident. He'd been alone at the farm when we called, so he had bundled you, still asleep, into the back seat. There, together, we learned your mother had died. It was a shock. I remember the three of us, in silence, watching you sleep, oblivious to the tragedy. I couldn't even cry. Your mother had just turned thirty-one. I went back to São Paulo with you, and your grandfather and your father stayed behind for the recovery of her body. Later, your grandfather told me your father was absolutely crushed, and that he might not even make it to the memorial service.

"While you lay asleep beside me, in my bed, still not knowing what had happened, I was waiting for your grandfather to call with more news. He only got home after dawn. The police in Monteiro believed your mother had lost control of the car and crashed off the cliff into the canyon.

"Later that day, while your grandad looked after preparations for the burial, I took you to the playground near the house. We'd decided that you would attend the funeral with us the next day, and that before allowing you to say goodbye to your mother at the religious ceremony, your father, grandfather, and I would give you the news. But you weren't yourself that day. When we got to the park, you didn't want to play with the other children. I remember sitting on those stone benches in front of the slides and swings, utterly drained, trying not to cry in front of you, when you came and sat beside me and said: 'Daddy was fighting with Mommy.'

"I thought perhaps you were talking about some fight that had happened during the separation, which had become very litigious. But you said it again. I started asking questions, and then I realized there was something strange about your mother's death—so I told your granddad. You told him the same story. There just happened to be a forensics expert who lived in our building. Your grandfather went to talk to him. They drove to Monteiro before your mother's funeral. Her car was still there because the forensics hadn't even got to it yet. When the pair of them arrived, along with the police officer from Monteiro, they analyzed the site of the accident and our neighbor spotted something that everyone had missed until then: the car key wasn't in the ignition.

"That was when the theory of the accident began to crumble. The next day, they carried out a full sweep of the area and the key was found in a gully, not far from the highway. Later they ran many more forensic examinations. There was no chance the key could have fallen from the dashboard and tumbled all the way to where it was found.

"Your father never admitted faking your mother's accident. But it was proven at the trial that, when he pushed her car off the edge, he forgot to put the key in the ignition. When he noticed his mistake, he simply tossed the key into the valley.

"But the definitive clue to the crime came from the forensics at the farm your father was renting. There were still some marks left from the blood you saw him mopping up. That's how we caught him," my grandma said.

"Who helped him?"

"A taxi driver from Monteiro, as we found out from a bank transfer your father made to him. He was also tried and sentenced as an accessory to the crime."

There were many more details I didn't know, and which my grandmother was able to explain. She said I would also be able to read all the documents from the trial, which she had kept somewhere in her house. One day perhaps I'd do that. But, seeing my grandmother's pain, I realized it wasn't worth taking the conversation further.

She placed her head on my shoulder and I breathed in her light, sweet perfume and stroked her gray hair. It felt like an epiphany: from now on, our roles were reversed. I would do more of the mothering, and she would be more of a daughter.

We went on holding hands, saying nothing. I looked out the window and saw the wide, transparent, cloudless sky outside. Below, the forest was a lush, intense green, the rivers like snakes twisting through it.

A wild and vivid beauty to feed the eyes and the soul.

X

ON THE STAGE, PAUL McCARTNEY was singing "I've just seen a face . . ." It wasn't easy to move in the crowd that was dancing and singing, transfixed, all around me.

I could hardly believe the length of the line for the bath rooms. I'd thought no one would be as crazy as me, going for a pee in the middle of the show, and I was already considering returning to join my friends when I saw, to the right of the stage, midway between the bar and the bathrooms, Amir kissing someone—she was really very pretty.

My first reaction was to make a swift exit, before he could spot me.

The week before, just as my lawyer initiated the case against him, I had gone live with thesimpleartofkillingawoman.com.

Back when I'd first had the idea, my plan had been just to establish the truth within my own professional circle, to tell my friends and acquaintances what Amir had done to me by filming our intimate moments without my consent, and how he had filled porn sites with his recordings, with the clear purpose of bringing about my moral assassination. But when I'd created the site, I ended up also telling the stories of my mother, Txupira, and Carla, and the stories of all the murdered women I'd been studying over the last few years. A journalist, a friend of a friend, had seen the site and written about it, and suddenly a stream of people had begun to visit it. That same afternoon, another reporter, working for a major television network, had called me to talk about thesimpleartofkillingawoman.com. Even so, the very last thing I wanted was to run slap-bang into Amir.

But then I saw he'd stopped kissing the pretty girl and gone off to the bar, and now suddenly the girl was behind me in the line for the toilets.

When my turn came, I went straight to the basins. I waited for her to go into the cubicle and waited for her to come out. While she was washing her hands, I took a tissue from the dispenser and offered it to her to dry them.

"Thanks," she said.

Then I plunged straight in, caution to the winds:

"That guy waiting for you outside . . . Amir . . . he—we used to go out . . . "

She looked at me in surprise. She smiled, more taken aback than curious.

"Take care," I said. "He physically assaulted me."

I got my phone and showed her my website.

"I'm bringing charges against him," I went on. "If you want to know more, it's all on this site."

She continued to stare at me; I think she was trying to work out whether or not to believe me. In the end she took my phone, looked at it for a brief moment, then gave it back.

"I thought you should know," I said, and left the bathroom. Outside, McCartney was playing the opening chords of "In Spite of All the Danger."

I threw myself into the crowd, aiming for my friends, my heart beating as if it was playing bass with the band. Suddenly, I felt an irresistible urge to hit the dance floor and move like there was only tomorrow.

ACKNOWLEDGMENTS

Writing books has always been a solitary activity for me. But it wasn't like that with *The Simple Art of Killing a Woman*. Throughout the time of its writing, I had the support and assistance of many professionals and friends to whom I would like to extend special thanks.

This book began with my editors Leila Name and Izabel Aleixo, who invited me to write a novel on any topic but with the essential ingredient of a female protagonist, and I accepted the challenge. Today I owe both of them far more than mere thanks for their reading, rereading, and discussion with me at each phase of the book's development, for their constant positivity and encouragement, and for providing the support as well as the freedom I needed to create this novel.

Without my friend, the journalist Emily Sasson Cohen, who shared the research for this book with me—interviewing dozens of specialists in violence against women, feminists, lawyers, indigenous leaders, and community leaders, as well as travelling to Acre to spend time in its jungle, to stand in for my eyes and ears—this book would not have been possible. Far more than a rigorous researcher, Emily is an active feminist, and her stance and commitment were crucially inspiring to the book.

Misha Glenny was likewise extremely generous in making available the interviews that he had carried out, along with Emily, for his novel *Nemesis*.

My interviews with Urso dos Santos, a teacher, cultural activist, tourist guide, and environmentalist, were of enormous assistance, as were those with child educationist Meyrinha Sorriso and cultural anthropology professor Carolina Grillo.

The list of people who helped us to understand the position of women in Acre (which had the highest femicide rate in Brazil at the time of this book's first publication) is also a long one, and I want to thank every one of them: Patrícia Rêgo, attorney at Acre's public prosecution office and director of their victims' helpline; public defender Cláudia Aguirre, who gave us a warm welcome both in court and in the jungle; and Shirley Hage, judge in charge of female protection cases, and her assistant Grazielle Outramário Wutzke. Acre-based public defenders Bruno Freitas and Rivana Ricarte de Oliveira; prosecuting attorney Diana Soraia Tabalipa; Eva Evangelista, high court judge on the TRE-Acre court and state coordinator of the Acrean organization for the protection of women in situations of domestic violence; and also their professional colleagues Eva da Silva Freire and Francisca Regiane da Silva Verçoza, interviews with whom provided valuable material for this book.

Terri Vale Aquino, anthropologist and founder of Acre's Pro-Indigenous Commission; journalist Altino Machado; Jairo Lima, regional coordinator of Funai in Cruzeiro do Sul and creator of the blog "Indigenous Chronicles"; the entire Puyanawa people and especially Luiz Puwe, Vari, cacique Joel, Maria Alice, and Evanízia Puyanawa, regional coordinator of Funai in Rio Branco; Letícia Yawanawá, coordinator of the Indigenous Women of Acre, southern Amazonia and north-east Rondônia branch; teacher Puruma Shanenawa (Eldo Carlos); journalist and writer Toinho Alves; Pajé Mutsá of the Katukina people; tourist guide Jackson Santos; indigenous specialist and regional coordinator of Funai in Dourados, Crizantho Alves Fialho Neto: all of their testimony and stories helped us to understand the tragic situation of indigenous people in Brazil today.

I am immensely grateful to my dear friends Beatriz Saldanha and Marcelo Piedrahíta for their many suggestions of material to read on Acre's origins, on the exploitation of the rainforest, and the position of women in Acre.

For those in São Paulo and Rio de Janeiro, the list of thanks is equally essential: I want to thank Gabrielle Piedade, a lawyer with Luiza Eluf; Lívia Gimenes, lawyer and professor of law at the University of Brasília; André Vieira Peixoto Davila, criminal investigator with São Paulo's Civil Police; and Renata Tavares Lessa, public defender in Rio de Janeiro.

Nicole Witt and Jordi Rocca have been far more than literary agents for me and this book, indeed it is difficult to imagine its ever existing without their shared enthusiasm and support.

Sophie Lewis translated the novel into English the way every author dreams: with the utmost knowledge, talent, and care.

ACKNOWLEDGMENTS

The enthusiasm and dedication of editor Jennifer Alise Drew and Restless Books were fundamental to bringing the book to English-speaking readers. Designer Sarah Schulte inspired our efforts with the creation of this very eye-catching cover.

It remains only for me to thank those friends who had the patience to discuss this subject with me, to show me pathways through it, to read my drafts and to send me their timely and invaluable observations. Thank you, then, Cláudio and Cornélia Rossi, Graziella Moretto, Pedro Cardoso, Renata Melo, and above all, my husband John Neschling, my daily inspiration, my most rigorous reader, my own personal editor, who reads everything over my shoulder, my eternal safe haven, who brings me back to the light every time I feel like giving up.

— PATRÍCIA MELO

I would like to thank Alison Gore for her enthusiasm in commissioning this translation and her support thereafter. Also at Restless Books, Jennifer Alise Drew for her sensitive and supportive editing. And Eduardo Leão, one-time lucky Restless intern, who has gone on to higher things but found the time to help immeasurably with terms relating to Brazilian indigenous community life. Thank you, too, to my friends Cide Piquet and Ramon Nunes Mello, you both helped me understand how to talk about the *tea*.

— SOPHIE LEWIS